Irish War Cry

Order of the Black Swan D.I.T. 3

The Department of Interdimensional Trespass

by

Victoria Danann

D.I.T. (Department of Interdimensional Trespass)

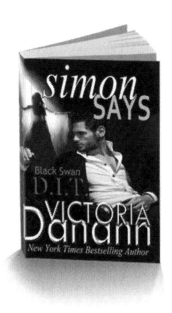

BOOK ONE

Director Simon Tvelgar is haunted by love that was lost but never fades with time. He thought she was gone forever, but what if…?

"Heart-warming, witty, quirky, a little racy and completely engaging!"

Rosie Storm is about to get the chance to head up a new Black Swan unit, D.I.T. The Department of Interdimensional Trespass.

Twenty years ago Sir Simon was a vampire hunter. He took three month's bereavement leave to go wild camping in the far north of Scotland following the death of his team leader. He expected solitude and fresh air to clear his mind and heart. He did not expect to fall in love. While wild camping on the stark landscape of the Orkney Islands, she disappeared into the standing stones. She faded into nothingness, a look of panic frozen on her face. As she reached out and silently called his name, he lunged to grab her an instant too late.

Her memory has haunted him every hour since.

Simon channeled his sorrow and loneliness into work until he eventually rose to the most powerful position ever held by an ex Black Swan knight. With tireless dedication, he built a congregation of talented misfits, watching and waiting for the one who could find Sorcha.

D.I.T. (Department of Interdimensional Trespass)

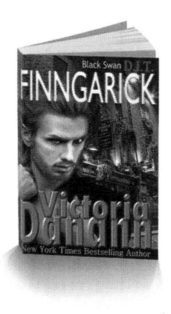

Book Two

- Torn Finngarick despises the phrase 'bad boy'.

- Sheridan O'Malley is on her way to becoming a Black
  Swan legend.

- Dublin is about to become a lot less demon-friendly.

"...a very fast-moving tale, twisting and turning like the

wildest rollercoaster." – *Night Owl Reviews TOP PICK*

When ex vampire hunting knight, Sir Torrent Finngarick, is hired by D.I.T., he's partnered with one of a pair of near-feral, New Forest elf twins who also happens to be his mate. Unfortunately Sher O'Malley made a pact with her twin when they were children that they would never accept a mate.

After rigorous training with Black-Swan-friendly demons and Black Swan knights emeritus, they're assigned to Dublin because there's an interdimensional stream portal somewhere in the vicinity of Trinity College and Temple Bar that's been causing havoc for centuries.

Just when Sher is succumbing to the inevitable pull of mating, she and Torn chase a trespasser through the portal underneath St. Patrick's. The wild redheaded beauty catches the demon's eye. And disappears.

PREFACE

AWOL

From the Memoir of Glendennon Catch

Sovereign Jefferson Unit, Order of the Black Swan

S IR TORRENT FINNGARICK stood in front of my desk looking like he'd just been dealt a mortal wound, but hadn't yet fallen because his brain hadn't quite caught up. Gods, I felt bad for the poor devil. Really bad.

He came to me hoping to call in every knight's ultimate marker. "I gave myself to The Order, risked my life every damn day. Now I need something I can't live without." It's the sort of favor you want to be able to say yes to before the question's even been asked.

Most of the time that's entirely possible. The Order is a prime mover in the world, connected financially and politically to every corner of the globe. There's little that can't be accomplished when a phone call is placed with precision.

But not this time.

Because the favor Finngarick needed wasn't of this world. Some fucking demon in another dimension had his girl. And my girl was almost as upset about it as he was.

If you hear a giant vacuum sucking sound, that's the audio backdrop for how I feel about this situation. There's not a thing I can do but leave this up to Kellareal and Deliverance and hope they've got enough game to set things right.

There's nothing I hate more than a feeling of power-lessness over an outcome. And that's where I am right now.

CHAPTER ONE

THE SOUND OF SILENCE

THE AIR FELT close around Torn. Pressing. In his mind he was struggling to breathe, but it was an illusion. His lungs were on an operating system independent of conscious thought. They continued to expand and contract regularly, faithful as a blacksmith's bellows.

He'd never spared a thought as to whether life or death was a choice.

By common standards his life wasn't great, but that was the hand he'd been dealt and he'd been committed to playing it out for better or worse. So he'd filled his time with Black Swan, women, drinking, and had experimented with drugs a couple of times. Drugs had bizarre effects on elves because of their heightened senses and neuro responses. So those were 'one offs'. His self-induced haze was mostly whiskey. Irish, to be exact.

It was simple. No need for days or weeks of contemplation or internal debate. If Sheridan was gone, he had no reason to continue.

Before she was taken, he'd reveled in four weeks of unbridled joy like a puppy playing in a field of spring wildflowers. Nothing about his reality had been unchanged. The air was clearer. Food tasted better. Colors were brighter. Sex was… hard to describe. Saying it was better was woefully inadequate. No matter how many years of debauchery he'd clocked, he'd never experienced the ecstatic sensual transcendent pleasure of mutual body, mind, soul connection.

After knowing what joy felt like, it was impossible to un-know it. Sitting on the edge of his bed in the darkness a laugh bubbled up and echoed around the room. It would be just like fate to show him what he was missing and then take it away.

It had been two weeks since Sher had fallen into the hands of a demon. A music demon. Or so he'd been told.

Rosie had offered to give him leave until she returned, but Torn had insisted that he needed work as a distraction.

He said, "I feel like, without work, I might just jump

right out of my body." She noted that he did look twitchy, unable to stay still for a minute. "I know that sounds daft. But 'tis how I'm feelin'."

"Hang on," Rosie told him. "I'm working on getting her back."

The first week Torn shied away from food, taking nourishment in the form of highly caffeinated 'energy' drinks whenever he began to feel 'off'. Since he didn't seem to be losing either vigor or muscle tone, he wasn't especially worried about the fact that hunger eluded him. By the end of the second week, he wasn't even moved to drink lightning-charged liquids. Why would he be? He didn't think about nourishment, got no satisfaction from it, and didn't seem to be suffering from the lack of food and drink.

He was consumed by a deep and abiding hunger.

But not for food.

For Sheridan O'Malley.

His attitude toward sleep was the same. It didn't interest him other than that he wished he could escape into the solace of unawareness it had once offered. Since he wasn't sleeping, he needed to find ways to fill his time. He dreaded being alone and could not abide silence.

He asked for double shifts monitoring the St. Patrick's portal and upped the ante by begging to work every day. He was desperate to fill the minutes that seemed to drag on forever with something other than need.

Eventually he drifted into a treaty born of shared misery with his mate's sister, Shivaun, and they began to form their own relationship. It seemed to give Shy comfort to talk about her twin and their lives growing up in the New Forest and Black on Tarry. That was fine with Torn because, as it happened, it gave him comfort to hear about those things. He and Sher hadn't been together long enough for him to hear all of her stories.

Being neck deep in the formation of a new Black Swan Unit, there'd been no time for honeymooning. No long lazy hours getting to know each individual freckle and hearing each and every story that made them who they were as individuals.

Torn had barely had a chance to ponder why the Powers That Be would have given someone like Sher a mate like him, before she was gone. From his vantage point she was deserving of nothing less than the finest, bravest, noblest elf in all of Ireland. But while he believed that truly in his heart of hearts, he wasn't returning the gift.

She was his.

And there was nothing that could get in the way of them being together.

Unless it was some rogue demon plucking her out of transit through the passes, no doubt because of her extraordinary beauty and the air of confidence she wore like custom made, body-fitting armor.

Since she had been taken, he went out of his way to avoid being alone, because his thoughts always turned to his own bad luck and whether or not it had rubbed off on Sher.

CHAPTER TWO

THE SOVEREIGN'S BOTTOM DRAWER

I N THE BOTTOM DRAWER of Glen's desk was a bottle of very special Irish whiskey that he kept on hand for late visits from Ram. When other members of A Team were away, he would stop by for surprisingly deep conversations on metaphysics and philosophy.

Once Glen made the mistake of asking, "Why are you here?"

Ram said, "Who do you think you're talkin' to like that? You may have these others fooled into believin' you're Sovereign of Jefferson Unit, but to me you're the dog walker."

Glen decided that being put in one's place occasionally was critical in promoting a balanced life and healthy attitude. So he made a point of stopping what he was doing, no matter how busy he was, to have a drink and a talk with the legend himself, whenever Ram came calling at his office door.

On that particular night, Ram noted that Glen looked more troubled than usual.

"Is the catastrophe impendin' or is it already here?" Ram asked as he leaned back in the armchair across from Glen's desk.

"What makes you think there's a catastrophe impending or otherwise?" Glen said.

"Known you since you were a teenage skirt chaser. That means I can read doom and gloom all over your pretty werewolf snout."

Glen turned the glass around in his hand. "Was that a racial slur?"

Ram snorted. "I have nothin' against werewolves and ye know it. Why are you dodgin' the question, Sovereign?"

"You know Sir Finngarick?"

"Oh, aye. I was no' fond of him after what he pulled at the Battle. I've ne'er felt like I could leave my family for my mother's birthday celebration since. But he did apologize and I had a chance to get to know him a little better durin' Rosie's trainin' camp." Ram scowled. "Why? Is he up to no good again?"

Glen shook his head. "No. Just the opposite. It turned out that his assigned partner was his mate."

"Know that. The women like to gossip." Glen smiled indulgently at that, having figured out somewhere along the way that men were even worse, but didn't correct the elf who'd been like a foster father. The good kind. "Seemed like a good match."

"Yeah. Problem is we lost her."

Ram shook his head slightly looking confused. "What do you mean lost her?"

"They were on assignment in Dublin. She disappeared in the passes. Now Finngarick is about to lose his mind."

Ram set the glass down on Glen's desk and leaned forward, elbows on his knees. "Great Paddy. I can no' begin to imagine the hel of that. 'Twould be torture."

"Yeah. Well. Rosie is in a tizzy. Finngarick is close to needing a straightjacket. And there's not a thing I can do about it."

"There is. If she's lost, we can look for her. Just like when Stormy…"

Glen was shaking his head. "Rosie's granddad and that

angel say word is that a demon's got her."

Ram, who'd been leaning forward, forearms resting on thighs, sat up straight looking considerably more worried. "What's that mean?"

"We're not sure yet. They're going to try to get her back, but apparently there are protocols."

"Protocols!"

"I know."

"Great Paddy."

"It's a music demon."

"A music demon? What the fuck is that?"

Glen waved his hand around. "I'm no expert. I'm just hearing about this and, at this point, you pretty much know what I know. Apparently we're manipulated through music all the time. By demons."

Ram looked worried. "Paddy," he said quietly as he considered that. "No' metal though?"

"Yeah. Metal, too." Glen laughed, but then sobered almost instantly. "Thing is," he looked at his glass and rotated it almost a full turn before speaking again, "it's not just Finngarick. The sister is almost as beside herself. I guess there's some mystical kind of bond thing with twins."

"There is." Ram nodded. "Elora and I have seen it over and over with our girls. It can be strange enough to weird you out. I can see how the one left behind would be feelin' crazy as a whirlin' dervish."

"What's a whirling dervish?"

"I do no' know. But my grandmum was fond of sayin' it. So even if 'twas no' a thing, 'tis one now."

"I'm going to write that down in my log of quotable Ram quotes."

Ram looked interested. "You keep a log of my sayin's?"

Glen laughed and shook his head. "No."

Sir Hawking shrugged that off and stood to leave. "Thanks for the whiskey. I better be gettin' home to the missus. She'll be wonderin' if I have a girlfriend."

He punctuated that with a wink, but both men knew perfectly well that mated elves define the term monogamous. Elora might be worried about whiskey consumption when he was out of sight. But the last thing she worried about was Rammel being attracted to someone else.

Turning back at the door. "If you change your mind

about a search party…"

Glen was nodding before Ram could finish the thought. "You'll be first call."

"Okay then."

CHAPTER THREE

THE DEMON'S DEN

"I BROUGHT YOU FOOD. Why aren't you eating?"

"No' hungry."

"Of course you are. Elves must consume food for fuel. It's part of the inferiority of your species." She glared at him. "Oh, sorry. I keep forgetting that you're sensitive about that."

"I can no' be sensitive about somethin' that is no' true. I simply think 'tis rude for you to insist on repeatin' the shite."

He laughed. "You are inferior, but it's so adorable when your color changes. Kind of chameleon-like."

"There's nothin' chameleon-like about it. I have fair skin…"

"And you anger easily."

She ignored that. "Chameleons change colors to

match the environment. Do you see anythin' pink in here?"

He smiled. "Just you."

"Exactly. So I ask you. Would a superior bein' get somethin' so simple so wrong?" He shrugged, smiling and completely undeterred. "Annnnnnd, I do no' anger easily."

"Seems so to me."

"Well, it *seems* you're wrong about that, too, then."

He laughed. "I'll bet your sister is not so much trouble."

She barked out a laugh. "Oh, demon, you have no idea. I'm a clump of clotted cream compared to Shivaun."

"Shivaun." Lyric turned the name over in his mouth like he liked the taste of it. "It's more musical than Sheridan."

"So what?"

The question dripped with suspicion and suddenly she was eager to steer the conversation in another direction. It was killing her to be separated from Torn, little by little, every day. But that was preferable to having her sister fall into the hands of the demon. She could have slapped herself for saying Shivaun's name out loud.

Even if he was astonishingly beautiful with the sexiest voice imaginable and also good at jigsaw puzzles, she was sure his windowless den was not the future Shivaun dreamed about. Although, since they'd promised each other to be celibate and unmated, they'd never allowed themselves to fantasize about lovers. Or, if they had, they'd never shared with each other. Even twins keep some secrets to themselves.

"Eat. I'm trying to take care of you."

She glared. "I'm no' a pet, demon."

He chuckled. "Well, you kind of are, elfess."

"Do no' call me that."

"What? Elfess?" He chuckled. "Why not? I rather like it. Makes me want to sing 'Jailhouse rock'."

"What?" It was clear that she didn't follow the reference.

"Never mind. But let me just say that, if I *did* sing 'Jailhouse Rock', you'd like it. A lot."

"Sure." She flopped onto one of the long divans and drummed her fingers on her thigh.

He cocked his head and studied her in that I-can-see-through-you way of his. "Did you sleep while I was gone?"

"What's it to you?"

That was ignored because he'd become distracted with a thought. He strode down the hallway that was defined by archways so smoothly curved they looked like beach art made from wet sand.

In a few seconds he was back. "You haven't used the facilities either."

"Now you've crossed a line. Bathroom usage is *personal. Way* personal."

"Whatever. What was the point of having me add a bathroom if you weren't going to use it?"

"Oh yeah! It was *so* much work. Was that your fourth finger that you crooked or your fifth?"

"Don't hate me because I can make things happen at will and you're a…"

She gave him a look that said, "If you finish that sentence, you're going to wish you were someplace else."

"Are you cold?" he asked.

With a flick of his wrist four arched fireplaces carved into smooth walls jumped to life. Even though there was no evidence of fuel, flames crackled and danced over glowing embers.

"Nice trick. No. I'm no' cold. I'm from the New Forest. 'Tis very far north which means we do no' get cold easily."

"No?"

"No."

"Even without vodka?"

Faint lines formed between her brows. "By now you should be gettin' the idea that I'm no' amusin' in any way. I'm plain and borin' and excruciatingly unentertainin'. So let. Me. Go."

He sat down on the divan across from where she sat. "You so underestimate yourself. I find you more fascinating than anything that's happened to me... well, maybe ever."

"'Tis ludicrous. Maybe I'll call you Ludicrous."

He shook his head. "My name is Lyric. And there's already a musician named, well, he doesn't know how to spell, but still, the idea is taken." Sher slapped both palms to her face in exasperation. "What was that?"

"This?" She did it again.

"Yes. That."

"It means I would run from the buildin' screamin' at

this point if only I could run from the buildin'."

"I can exchange you for Shi…"

"Do no' say her name."

"The interrupting is becoming tedious. Why not?"

"Because you get this funny look on your face like you're thinkin' about masturbatin'. And I just do no' want to see that."

He laughed out loud. "I can't imagine why you think you're not amusing." His eyes drifted to the Chinese takeout cartons that sat on the large low table between them. "Is it that you don't like Chinese?"

She looked down at the little white cartons with wire handles and red calligraphy symbols on the sides. Sheridan was a recent convert, since she'd never had Chinese until a few weeks before, but she liked it. Of course. Everybody likes some kind of Chinese and it looked like Lyric had brought a variety buffet.

She did like Chinese. And she hadn't eaten for what was probably… "How long have I been here?"

"In Loti time? Two weeks."

"I think that's impossible," she said, just realizing that she hadn't been eating or sleeping or using the new bath facilities.

As if Lyric really could read her mind, he said, "I'm not an expert, but I believe it's not possible for elves to go so long without food, drink, sleep, and…" He glanced toward the hall that led to the bath, but didn't want to offend unnecessarily by bringing up such a sensitive subject. Again.

CHAPTER FOUR

THE WILD BUNCH

ONE BY ONE the hunters began to notice little changes. The day-to-day change was so minute and so gradual that they didn't notice until the effect was smack-you-in-the-face cumulative.

One day after a hot shower Torn swiped at the fog that had formed on the bathroom mirror. It was steamy enough in the room that it formed again almost as fast as he wiped it away. But something out of place caught his eye. He leaned in closer, turned the towel to find a drier spot, swiped again, and… there it was.

He stepped back like he'd been stung. Then looked around reflexively even though he knew he was alone.

There was no question about it. He was still himself, just more. In the best way possible.

His hair had always been on the darker side of ginger

with overtones of light brown, but what he was seeing in the mirror was the deep crimson color of red maple leaves in autumn. He toyed with the idea that he might be playing mind games with himself, but no. His eyes were unmistakably a new value of blue. The color wasn't darker. Just more intense.

His skin looked luminous, also flawless. He checked the inside of his forearm where he'd been slashed deep with a broken bottle in a bar fight. No scar.

Likewise he ran a hand over the slightly raised scar that had run crisscross across his abs for the past seven years, thanks to a vamp with too-long nails. Raif's wife, before she was his wife, had suggested scar-reduction cream, but he'd never really seen the point of trying to disguise the physical events that punctuated his experience. He ran his hand over his torso again.

Moot point.

The skin was smooth and perfect as a newborn baby. Not a freckle or pore or blemish to be found. Anywhere. Much less scarring.

He dressed quickly and headed downstairs.

Shy and Deck were in the breakfast room. Not eating

breakfast.

"How long has it been since you've eaten?" he asked.

"What?" Shivaun said, looking over at Declan. "Why are you asking?"

"Just answer," Torn insisted. "Did you have breakfast?"

"No, I…" said Shy.

"Supper last night?"

"No," she answered.

"Lunch yesterday?"

"What are you getting at, Torn?" Declan interjected, beginning to look uncomfortable with the direction of the questioning.

Torn turned his attention to Deck. Declan had the dark hair and blue eyes of his ancestors, the Fingal. He didn't get much of a tan herding reindeer. And he certainly didn't spend time in the sun in Ireland. Yet there he sat with smooth and perfect skin bearing the warm glow of tan that Torn knew was the stuff of sexual magnetism.

"Been sunbathing, Deck?"

"You sleepwalking, Finngarick? Your questions are…"

"Disturbing?" Torn said.

"I was going to say haywire," Deck finished.

"Call it what you want. Fact remains we're changed. Look at your partner. Her hair has turned red in a way that does no' happen in nature. And her eyes. She did no' used to have those gold flecks in her eyes."

Torn felt a twinge in his heart wondering if Sheridan was changing as well. Would she look different when she was returned?

Shivaun picked up a lock of hair that had fallen forward over her breast and raised it to eye level. After examining it, she turned to study Deck. "You do look more…"

"Yeah?"

She shook her head and made a helpless gesture with her hands. "More."

"I look more more?" Deck asked. "Well, now that that's cleared up. Let's go to work." Deck stood up.

"No' so fast," Torn said. "I'm no' done."

"I say you are."

Declan seemed ready to change the subject. But Finngarick was determined to finish what he'd begun and let it be known, partly by the steady gaze he leveled at Deck and partly by the fact that his tone of voice said he'd made up his mind.

"No. I'm no'."

"Wait," Shy said. "Let's have a listen. I want to hear this."

Deck sat back down and crossed his well-muscled arms over his abs. "I guess you have the floor, brother."

"You can be in denial if you want, Deck. But somethin' has happened. We're changin'. You're no' eatin'. When was the last time you slept?"

Deck and Shivaun both stared at Torn like they were afraid of what he was going to say next. When they pulled their gaze away they gave each other a worried glance.

"What are ye sayin'?" Shivaun asked.

"We're no' sleepin', eatin', drinkin', and we look different, but that's no' all. We're fast."

"Well, of course we're fast. Black Swan doesn't take on little old ladies to be hunters," Deck said.

Torn nodded. "You have no' noticed that we're movin' faster in the passes?"

"Practice. That's all," Deck said. "We're gettin' better."

"Yeah. We're gettin' better because we're becomin'

somethin' else. Or maybe we already are somethin' else."

Deck frowned. "Like what? Just say what's on your mind."

Torn shook his head. "Nothin' doin'. I want you to name it."

"Name what?"

There was a knock on the door.

"That's the post fella," Deck said.

"Okay. Come with me," Torn said.

Shy and Deck both got up and followed.

Torn answered the door. "Fine mornin', Doo."

As Shy and Deck looked on the postman opened his mouth to return Torn's greeting, but they saw Torn turn and walk back to the kitchen.

"Hey. Where'd he go?"

Shy and Deck looked at the postman. "Torn?"

"Yeah. Who else would I be talkin' about?"

"Did you no' see him leave?" Shy asked.

The postman narrowed his eyes. "This some kind of practical joke? The elf was here, then he was no'. Simple as that. Did ye no' see the same thing?"

"Oh, yeah, we did," said Deck.

"'Tis a trick of the light," said Shy. "A new toy Torn's been playin' with. Thought he'd have you on."

"Ah." Doo smiled faintly. "Well, tell him he got me good."

Deck took the mail and said, "Thanks. We will."

When he shut the door, Torn walked into the front room with his hands in his back pockets. "See?"

"See what, Torrent?" Deck asked. "Tell me what we just saw."

"Did you see me leave the room?" Torn asked the two of them.

"Aye. O'course," Shy answered.

"'Tis o'course to you. But no' to him." Torn jerked his chin toward the door where Doo had been a minute before. "To him it just looked like I vanished."

He waited.

Finally Deck said, "And?"

"For Paddy's sake, man. Who else do you know who's got flawless good looks and can travel so fast he vanishes right before your eyes?"

Shy sucked in a sharp gasp. "Demons," she whispered.

Torn looked from Deck to her. "That's right. Demons.

That serum did no' just alter us a little. It altered us a lot. I think we're demons."

"That's ridiculous!" Deck said.

Shivaun looked at her partner. "We're no' happy about it either, Declan. But sayin' 'tis no' so does no' change a thing." She held his gaze then added, "I admit it. You look good, the both of you."

"What are you plannin' to do?" Deck said.

Torn sighed, looked down at the floor then slowly began to smile.

"What's funny?" Shy said.

He looked up. "Let's go for a test drive."

"What do you...?" Deck started, but seeing Shivaun's answering smile he stopped mid-sentence and looked between the other two.

Shy grinned. "Aye. Let's find out what the new and improved versions can do."

Before Deck could protest, Torn had left the building with Shivaun right behind.

"Do you see what I see?" Torn asked the two of them. Finngarick discovered that, if he let his eyes drift slightly out of focus, he could see slight changes in his surroundings. Like pockets of fog quickly coming and going. He had the thought that they looked something like mystic geysers.

Shy and Deck stopped and looked around to see if they could pick up on what he meant.

"Are those...?" Shivaun raised a finger to point.

Finngarick grinned. "Guess there's only one way to find out."

"Aw. Wait a minute," Deck said, but before he had a chance to make his protest heard, Torn and Shy had already stepped into one of the foggy-looking shapes and disappeared. If he hesitated, he wouldn't be able to find them. So he followed just as that shape was fading. A second later and it would be gone.

The two other hunters were waiting in the passes. Torn's new inexplicable senses informed him that, if he stepped back out exactly where he'd come in, he wouldn't find himself outside the D.I.T. house in Dublin. The grid that formed the passes was, apparently, always in motion.

He had a momentary worry, wondering how he'd find his way back, but discovered that, as soon as he thought about the house in Dublin, he knew exactly how to get there. He knew he wouldn't be heard if he tried to talk to the others in the passes because there was a whirring noise, like a desert wind, that would drown out his voice. So he motioned for them to follow.

When the three arrived at their starting point, none the worse for wear, Deck said, "Okay. That was kind of trippy."

"You mean because it did no' feel alien?" Shy said.

"Yeah. I guess that is what I mean." Deck's eyebrows rose. "Are you creeped out? I'm creeped out."

"I have a feelin' that 'tis no longer appropriate to be 'creeped out', brother. 'Cause we may just be the creepies now."

"Not sure I like hearing that," Deck advised.

"Why'd you bring us back here?" Shy said. "I thought we were goin' to find out what we can do with these changes."

Torn nodded. "We are. I want to head over to the portal at St. Patrick's. Find out what's the difference between accessin' the passes this way and that way."

Shivaun nodded. "Aye. Good idea. Let's go."

WHEN THEY STEPPED through the portal underneath St. Patrick's they immediately understood the difference. Whereas the 'geyser' they'd entered by the house had given them access to a pass that was like a narrow hallway, the portal at the cathedral opened into a wide passageway that would be more like an avenue than a hallway. It was a hub corridor with dozens of exits, arched openings outlined with borders of light.

Unlike the murky fog of the passes, this avenue looked more like the inside of a vast cavern with indirect lighting. It gave the impression that it was lined with shops and restaurants, but this was a mirage. In fact the openings could lead to anything; shops, restaurants or worlds only dreamt of in the imaginations of fantasy artists.

Whereas the D.I.T. hunters' forays through the portal had previously been fruitless, they now saw that the avenue was rather busy with all manner of elementals busily coming and going on some errand or another. Most gave the three of them, particularly Shivaun, curious looks as they passed, but they didn't slow or stop on their way by.

Shivaun looked at Finngarick with wide eyes that

clearly said, "What. The. Hel?"

He shook his head and shrugged. For several minutes they remained where they were, more or less fascinated by the spectacle that few, if any, other elves or humans had ever witnessed. At length, when they'd looked their fill, Torn motioned for them to reenter Loti through the portal.

Back on the other side, in the reality that they thought of as 'home', Torn said, "Great Paddy. That place is crawlin' with ooglie booglies."

Deck smirked. "Like you said, who are we to judge? We're the ooglie booglies now." He didn't look especially happy about that. "You think they've been in there all along?"

Torn gave Deck a pointed look. "Do no' play dumb with us, Deck. You know they were there. We just could no' see 'em before."

Deck took in a deep breath.

Shivaun said, "We need to call Rosie."

Torn's eyes flicked to Shy. "Got a better idea."

"Somehow I already know I'm not gonna like it," Deck said.

"Stop bein' such an old woman!" Shy told Declan. To Torn, she said, "What's your idea?"

Finngarick smiled. "We're goin' to show her."

ROSIE WAS IN her closet trying to decide what to wear to dinner in New York with her husband. It was date night and just what the doctor ordered. It had been a long week of D.I.T. administration details and being on a different schedule than Glen's. Looking in the tilt mirror, she thought the crimson silk blouse from Bergdorf might be too low cut to wear to dinner in New York. It hadn't looked quite so scandalous when she bought it. She didn't remember it revealing this much skin.

She thought she might have felt the prickle of sense awareness that other demons were nearby, but dismissed it as a sign that she needed a more intense moisturizer.

She put the blouse back on the hanger and stepped into her bedroom wearing just underwear. It took a lot to scare a witch/demon, but when Rosie found three hunters standing in her room, she jumped and squealed. At the same time, the occupants of Jefferson Unit thought they might have felt a minor earthquake, but when the tremor disappeared so fast, they concluded it was their imagination.

Rosie grabbed one of Glen's tee shirts hanging on the door next to her. As she was pulling it over her head, she said, "WHAT THE MOTHER OF ALL FUCKING FUCKS ARE YOU THREE DOING IN MY BEDROOM?!?"

She did not look pleased.

Torn spoke up. "We're sorry to surprise you. We just thought it would be easier to show, rather than try to explain, that there's been a new development."

Rosie looked between the three of them. Having gotten over the shock of finding people in her bedroom, she was beginning to think more clearly. Sir Torrent Finngarick, Shivaun O'Malley, and Sir Declan Tikkenen were supposed to be in Dublin.

"Wait for me in the living room." She pointed toward the door.

On the way out, Deck said, "Purple's my favorite," referring to her lingerie.

Shivaun slapped him in the ribs. "Sorry," she told Rosie. "We're workin' on socialization."

In less than two minutes, Rosie was in her living room wearing a tee shirt that read "*Everybody* could *not* have been Kung Fu fighting" and khaki capris. The three hunters were standing in the middle of the room.

"Sit down," she said. "And talk."

Torn and Shy sat on the sofa. Deck took one of the big upholstered chairs.

"Like I said," began Torn, "there's been a development. We do no' have an explanation. Conjecture that somehow the serum is doin' a better job than expected? Maybe? In any case, we do no' need devices to find our way through the, erm, passes. Anymore."

"And we look good," Shy said.

Rosie turned her attention to Shivaun. They had all been good-looking by any standard before. But now that it was mentioned, she could see what Shivaun meant. They were no longer beautiful in the way that humans and elves are beautiful. They were beautiful in the way that elementals are beautiful, which meant they were flawless. Like they, themselves, had been airbrushed and color enhanced.

"You do," Rosie confirmed calmly. "Tell me *exactly*

how you found your way here."

Torn, Shy, and Deck looked at each other. When no one else spoke, Torn said, "Just thought about you. Ended up here."

"I see," Rosie said in a tone as matter-of-fact as if they'd recited the grocery list. "What else have you noticed?"

"We can see these things." Torn looked at the other two hunters. "They're kind of like little towers of mist and they're always comin' and goin'. We stepped into one and it was a pass. So we went over to St. Patrick's to see how the portal is different."

"Great Paddy, Rosie. 'Tis full of busy creatures comin' and goin'. We could no' see 'em before." She looked between Torn and Deck. "Which seems impossible because we've been workin' there for weeks. I guess you have to be one of 'em to see 'em 'cause they're movin' so fast."

Rosie nodded her head absently, trying to sort through what this would mean to the program, but she was also trying to rein in the excitement about how it might serve D.I.T. to have demon hunters who were actually *demon* hunters because there was a larger issue.

Sounding far more like Monq than she intended, she heard herself asking, "And how do you feel about this?"

"Well," Shy said. "I'm kind of okay with it. I do no' see a downside as of yet. I do no' need to eat, drink, or sleep. And this, um, condition would obviously help me do the job I'm supposed to be doin'."

"In fact, given what we saw in the portal, there's a chance that we ne'er would have been able to do the job," Torn added.

Rosie studied them for a minute. "You seem to be making an adjustment. Faster than I would have expected. But I guess adaptability is one of the qualities we test for when looking for Black Swan candidates. So maybe that's not so surprising."

She sighed and drummed her fingers on the arm of her chair. "We don't know if this effect is temporary or permanent. How do you feel about that?"

Shivaun looked at her partner, who shrugged. "Either way. I guess we'd better keep the necklaces with us just in case it wears off when we're workin'."

"True enough," Torn said. "So. What are we?"

"You're mimicking the abilities of elementals," Rosie said. "Since you were given serum with demonic properties, I think we have to assume you're demons. But again, we don't know if that's temporary or not."

"Hypothetical," Torn said. "Let's just say 'tis permanent. What would that mean to us?"

Rosie wiggled her head on her shoulders. "Well, it would mean that you could expect to live a really really long time. You won't need a salary because you can always find a way to do anything you want, have anything you want. Within reason. The question is, will you still fulfill your commitment to work for D.I.T.?"

"O' course," Shivaun said. "What do you take us for?"

"Aye," said Torn. "I do no' see spendin' eternity goin' through car magazines."

Rosie looked at Deck. He said, "Yeah. I'm in for keeps."

"This is going to cause quite a stir in Black Swan."

Torn nodded. "I expect so. And, if we're expressin' these traits, 'tis safe to say the others are as well."

"Yes." Rosie nodded. "You're right. Looks like D.I.T. has just accidentally evolved into something we couldn't have imagined."

"What's next?" Torn asked.

After taking in a deep breath and releasing it, Rosie said, "Guess I'm going to need to gather your brethren at the Abbey for a guess-what-you-might-be-demons-now meeting." She looked them over. "By the way, Shy is right. You do look good."

"What about Sher?" Torn said. "If she's like us, can we no' just go get her?"

Rosie pursed her lips. "We're very close to having that done, Torn. Just be patient a little longer. We'll have her back and avoid an interdimensional inter-species incident."

Torn's brows drew together. "Patient. You do no' know what you're askin."

"You're right. I don't. It won't be much longer. If we don't have her back in two days, I'll go get her myself."

"Can I hold you to that, boss?" Torn asked, looking slightly encouraged.

"You can, sir knight." She softened her voice. "You're going to get her back."

Torn looked like he wanted nothing more than to believe her.

"Now you three need to get out of here. I have arrangements to make. Oh. And keep this between us until I get everybody to the Abbey. I want to have everyone gathered so that all questions can be handled at once." The guests rose to leave. "One more thing. There are some basic guidelines about where and when you show up unannounced. Underwear is one thing, but that's not the only thing that goes on in that room." She pointed toward her bedroom.

With a jaunty sort of smirky smile, Torn said, "Understood." Growing more serious, he said, "Maybe you can teach us how to avoid such things. I just thought about you and there I was."

"Okay. I'll make a list of things to cover at the Abbey."

"About that…" Torn said. Rosie gave him her attention. "I'd like permission to stay behind in Dublin. I mean just in case. What if the, erm, demon brought Sher back? I would no' want her to come to an empty house."

"Alright. It's not like you don't already know the score. You stay behind. You two," she looked at Shy and Deck, "need to be there to relate your experiences with the slips and the portal."

"Slips?" Deck asked.

"Oh. That's what we call those things that look like, what did you say? Misty towers?"

SHE PULLED HER PHONE from a thigh pocket on her cargo pedal pushers and called Grieve.

"Aye, madam?"

"Grieve, I need everybody gathered at the Abbey. Right away."

"By everybody, you mean the hunters?"

"That's right. Have them there for dinner tonight at eight. That is, if the kitchen staff can pull together food in that time frame."

Since the Abbey was no longer occupied to capacity, there was no need to keep a full complement of food service workers.

"I'm certain they can manage. Will the hunters be spendin' the night?"

She thought about that for a minute. "As a matter of fact. Tell them to come prepared to spend a couple of nights."

"Very good, madam."

"Alright. I'm leaving now. If you have trouble arranging transportation for anybody, let me know."

"I shall."

ROSIE SHOWED UP in Glen's office unannounced.

"To what do I…?" he began.

"We have a situation."

"Oh?"

"Oh. Yeah. Listen to this."

She briefed Glen because, technically, he was Monq's boss, directly responsible for him. Protocol directed that Glen be informed first.

Rosie knew her husband well enough to know that he was seething by the time he rose from his chair. The fact that he was going to the sublevel labs personally instead of demanding that Monq make an immediate appearance in the office spoke volumes.

As Glen stomped toward the elevator she followed along after like a kid who's tattled and, perversely, wants to see the consequences about to be rained down on the accused.

He stormed into the lab where Monq was lecturing a couple of assistants about something. Everybody looked up. Rosie hung back, holding the door open.

Glen pointed at Monq and didn't try to disguise his fury. "Your office. Now."

Glen's tone of voice was so low, calm, and steady that, oddly, it was scarier than if he'd been yelling. But the yelling wasn't far behind.

As soon as the door of Monq's office closed him in with Glen and Rosie, Glen rounded on Black Swan's own resident renaissance man. "WHAT HAVE YOU DONE NOW?"

Monq blinked. "Pardon?" He didn't seem flustered, or even bothered, by the anger directed his way, just curious as to the cause.

"Sit down," Glen directed. Monq started to move behind his desk. "Not there. Here."

Glen pointed to an armchair.

Monq sat.

"What's this about, Sovereign?" Monq asked, flicking

a glance at Rosie and noting that, while she wasn't as mad, she wasn't wearing her typical cheerful face either. She looked grave.

"Your serum that was supposed to enable Rosie's hunters to access the passes and increase their speed and reaction time? The Deliverance serum?"

"Yes. What about it?"

"It didn't enable the hunters to temporarily mimic demon traits. IT TURNED THEM INTO DEMONS!"

Monq looked genuinely shocked, a benchmark of sorts because Monq didn't surprise easily. "What?!?"

"You heard me. Another Monq-saves-the-world solution gone awry."

Monq cocked his head as he looked up at Glen standing over him and over at Rosie leaning against the door like she was making sure no one got in or out.

"Well, that's one way to look at it," Monq offered.

"One way to look at it," Glen repeated drily. "You are not about to tell me you think this is a good thing. If you even try that, you're fired."

"It is kind of a good thing."

"You're fired."

Monq ignored that. "I understand that it could be seen as questionable, but on the other hand, you could say that The Order now has sixteen demons working for Black Swan. Could be just what the doctor 'ordered'." He chuckled, delighted by his own joke.

"You have turned the bend into mad scientist territory, you crazy old bastard." When Monq responded with a smile, Glen said, "I am not being funny. Did you or did you not know that this could happen?"

Monq was shaking his head. "No. It's something none of us even considered." He brightened. "But you have to admit it's exciting."

"Not only do I not have to admit anything of the sort, but I'm fairly astonished that you'd have the nerve to use the word 'exciting'."

"Why? Think of the possibilities."

Glen could tell by looking at Monq that his mind was already busy thinking up schemes to make people extra-mortal.

Glen half sat, half leaned on the outer edge of Monq's enormous desk, with its elaborate carving. A couple of centuries before some German family had spent an entire winter carving that desk. Glen lifted his butt where a dragon brow was digging in and resettled a couple of inches over.

He modulated his tone, thinking he could get through to Monq with reason. "Do you understand that there are now sixteen baby demons who weren't asked whether or not they wanted to give up their people papers? Has it occurred to you that we don't know what the side effects might be? It could kill every one of them because their bodies weren't designed for the stress of demon speed and strength. It could jimmy their brain chemistry and turn them into the sort of psychopaths that even nightmares can't touch. Try to imagine the havoc that an insane demon could cause."

Monq didn't look particularly worried about Glen's concerns. "Do we know whether it's temporary or permanent?"

Glen looked at Monq like he was talking to a child. "No," he said, with exaggerated patience. "We're hoping that *you* can establish that."

"Sure." Monq nodded. "How?"

"No. 'How' is *my* question. Not *yours*. You're the one

who made this mess. You're the one who's going to clean it up."

"Clean it up?"

"Yes. Clean. It. Up."

"What do you mean by that? Exactly."

"Criminently." Glen threw up his hands, his shoulders sagged, and he looked away wondering why in the world he'd taken a job that involved supervising a brilliant lunatic.

Rosie took those gestures as a tag team signal and turned the conversation into a trialogue. "So far I've talked to three of those affected. It appears they will make an adjustment, although I think they're still in shock and haven't considered all the implications. Like, for instance, that they have stopped aging while their families will continue to grow old and die. Like that, unlike elementals who were created *naturally*, they don't have an actual place in the scheme of things. A job!"

"They have a job with Black Swan."

"Making my point. We're monkeying around with things we shouldn't be."

"Oh for gods' sake, Elora."

VICTORIA DANANN

"Elora *Rose*," she corrected.

"Yes. Yes. Elora Rose. The whole don't-mess-with-nature argument has plagued science, probably since some lazy fella thought up the wheel. Progress requires experimentation. I grant you that sometimes there are unexpected results."

At that Glen turned and gave Monq a withering look.

Monq was either oblivious or undaunted. "But this isn't a tragedy. It's a happy accident! You're not considering the benefits."

"Since you're already fired and are not going to get the opportunity to implement these 'benefits' as you see them, go ahead and lay it out for us."

"Well, for one thing, we could put an end to the vampire virus."

Glen barked out a laugh. "Yeah? We've heard that one before. Right?"

Monq wagged his head back and forth and waved at the air. "Just listen. If all the vampire hunters were injected, they'd be truly immunized. There would never be another fatality. And with the increased speed, and ability to appear out of nowhere, I'm guessing they could rid the world of vampire in…" He stopped and appeared to be calculating internally, "less than two weeks."

Glen's gaze flicked to Rosie. Monq was playing the morally ambivalent genie who offered what was most desired in all the world with the catch that it would be acquired by questionable means.

Rosie saw that Glen was thinking that through. Considering the ramifications. It was highly unlikely that someone in his position would ever face a more seductive, tempting dilemma in the guise of a proposal. She knew the moment Glen cleared his head of fantasies about ending the scourge once and for all and returned to the heart of the matter. She recognized the slight straightening of his shoulders, the set of his jaw, and the determined steadiness of his gaze. He'd made up his mind.

"We're not in the business of genetic engineering, Dr. Monq. We are in the business of taking care of our people. *Ethically.*" The last word intended to be heard as punctuation to a philosophy. "Find out whether or not this is permanent."

Glen left no doubt that the debate was concluded. Rosie looked back once as she followed Glen out the door.

Monq raised his eyebrows. What that meant, she couldn't say.

In the hallway, on the way to the elevator, Rosie said, "You want a glass of wine?"

Glen stopped in his tracks. Normally he would thank her, but say he was in the middle of a work day that would never end if he took a break. On that particular occasion, he surprised her by saying,

"Yeah. Okay."

Her eyes widened slightly as her lips curled up. She linked arms with him and said, "Hold on tight. I know just the place."

"Rosie. Wait a…"

He was in the passes before he could finish the sentence. A few minutes later they stood on the terrace of the vintner villa where Glen's in-laws lived.

"I know this place." He smiled.

"Oh yeah?" She laughed. "I hear they make a mean glass of wine. And the weather is perfect for sitting on the terrace."

Glen looked around. "You have the best ideas."

"And don't forget it," she quipped.

A pickup truck pulled up just as Rosie turned to go in the house. Storm got out and slammed the door.

"Daddy!" She never got tired of greeting him like she was still a child. He never got tired of hearing her do it. She gave him a big squeeze. "I didn't know you'd be here. I brought Glen for a glass of Black Swan on the terrace. He's having a very bad day."

"Oh?" Storm looked over at Glen.

"Come join us and we'll tell all," Rosie said, although it was more a demand than a request.

"Who could refuse a tell-all offer?" Storm said.

"And you can talk one sovereign to another."

Storm looked at Glen. "Oh. *That* kind of a bad day, is it?"

While Rosie was fetching glasses and wine, Storm tossed his hat on the table and sat down. He didn't need a hat. His demon genes made it impossible for his skin to burn or sustain damage of any kind from weather. Physically he was probably in his late twenties, but the experiences he'd collected showed on his face and his bearing, making him appear somewhat older.

"What's up?" Storm asked.

"Rosie's sixteen hunters? Her D.I.T. crew?"

"Yeah?"

"Monq has turned them into demons."

Whatever administration snafu Storm had been expecting to hear about, that wasn't it. He sat back in his chair slack jawed, wondering if there was any chance it was a joke.

Like he was mind reading, Glen said, "And no. I'm not kidding."

"You mean full-fledged, real deal demons? Like Deliverance?"

Glen took in a deep breath and moved his head in a circle. "No testing has been conducted, but according to what Rosie says, yeah. Full-fledged, real deal. Like Deliverance."

Storm was scrubbing a hand down the front of his face when Rosie arrived.

"I see you've already told him," she said. "How's he taking it?"

"Don't know yet," Glen said as if Storm wasn't there. "Any minute he's going to speak."

"I take it this was an accident."

Glen gave Rosie a nervous glance. "Honestly, until just now, it hadn't occurred to me that it might be deliberate. I mean, Monq can be a royal fuck up, as we all know, but he wouldn't go rogue scientist. Would he?"

Storm looked at Rosie, who shrugged. "I'd like to say it wasn't intentional, but he seemed so damn pleased about it."

"You know what they say about a thin line between genius and crap crazy," Storm proffered. His eyes moved from watching the wine pour to Rosie. "How are they taking it?"

"The hunters?"

"Yeah."

"I've only seen three. I'm meeting with the rest tonight at the Abbey in Scotia. I'm not sure the rest of them know. I think Finngarick kind of figured it out like a puzzle. He may be more observant than most."

Storm harrumphed. "Who would have guessed that?"

"I take it from your tone that you don't like him?" Rosie asked. Storm just took a sip of wine and declined to answer. "Why?"

"Why?" He looked at his daughter like she needed to

get a clue. "Rosie. The elf is good for nothing. He botched his life. Botched every assignment he was ever given. I'm pretty sure Black Swan would have loved to get a resignation letter."

Rosie cocked her head. "Maybe he's changed."

"Uh-huh." Storm looked unconvinced.

"Well, he's not botching D.I.T. Matter of fact, his team seems to look up to him."

"In what way?"

"Well, when they came to see me, I'd ask a question and they'd look to him to answer."

"Sound familiar?" Glen asked Storm.

Storm shrugged. "When it really counted, he let Elora and everybody else at Jefferson Unit down."

"Whoomp! There it is!" Rosie said to Glen as she threw her hands up in the air. "Might have known that if you've got a beef with somebody we could trace it back to Elora."

Storm gaped and then clenched his jaw. "Do you have something to say?"

"I guess not."

"What does that mean?"

"It means I got your memories up to the time I was conceived. Remember? I know you were in love with Elora. And I know Mom was worried you always would be."

"But you don't have the memories we've made since then, do you?"

"No."

"Rosie. Your mom and I are solid as it gets. If she thought I was in love with Elora, Elora wouldn't be her best friend."

"He has a point," Glen put in.

Storm looked at Rosie with a newfound curiosity. "Have you been worried about this your whole life?"

"Well, sort of," she said.

Storm's face softened. "You should have said something sooner. The way I felt about Elora was a thimble of moisture in the ocean of love I have for your mother. Litha wasn't a consolation prize. She was a trade up."

Rosie immediately misted over. "Really?"

Storm held up two fingers in some kind of mock pledge. "Demon's honor."

"Oh. Ha. Ha," she said.

He smiled. "You've got more important things to do than worry about your parents' love lives. If it means so much to you, I'll keep an open mind about the new improved Finngarick."

"You should. He's mated to his partner. And she was abducted in the passes. By a music demon."

"What in gods' name is a music demon?"

"That's what I said," Glen put in before draining the last of his glass. "You guys are making good wine here. We'll take a case. Matter of fact, J.U. will take ten cases."

"You're late to the party," Storm said. "We already have a contract with every Black Swan unit in the world."

"Who authorized that?"

Storm chuckled. "You really want to talk about wine requisitions?"

"No. I really want to talk about what to do about Monq."

"Yeah. That's the question." Storm glanced between Rosie and Glen. "If he did it deliberately, he has to go. And that's no small thing because the man is a Black Swan institution."

"When he laid out the possibilities, there was a moment…"

"What are you talking about?"

"He said, you know, that he could give the vampire hunters the same serum. It would make them immune so that not a single knight would ever die at the hands of a vamp again. And it'd also make the hunters so fast that they'd be able to wipe out vampire, all vampire. He said in two weeks."

Storm looked at Rosie. She nodded confirmation.

Storm's eyes glazed over as Glen's had imagining what the world would be like with no vampire. "Hard to walk away from that."

"I know. I told him we're not in the genetic engineering business."

"You did the right thing. So why do you still look worried?"

"I'm wondering if I can take responsibility for this decision or if I need to kick it upstairs."

"Simon?" Glen nodded. "You're in charge of Monq."

"Yes. But it's kind of a technicality, only because he chooses to live near New York. In fact, he's The Order's version of science at large."

Storm looked at Rosie. "You think he should take this to Simon?" She shook her head. "Why not?"

"Just between us?" Storm and Glen both nodded. "Simon is so close to the D.I.T. project. Because of Sorcha. It's personal with him. I don't know that it would cloud his judgment, but it might."

"And what?" Glen said. "You think he might order Monq to start converting employees to demons so that he can keep aliens out of Loti?"

She took a sip of wine. "Crossed my mind. Yes."

"There's your answer," Storm said. "If this circles round, I'll back you up on the decision."

Glen nodded. "Thanks. Appreciated." He sighed. "Meanwhile, I've told Monq to find out if the effect is temporary or permanent."

"Good. So what's the problem?"

"I have this awful feeling that he might strike off on his own. You should have seen how animated he looked when he started talking about making more demons."

"Keep a close eye. If you get any hint that he's stepping outside the lines, I'll get involved and go to Simon with you."

Glen stood and shook Storm's hand. "Thanks, Dad."

Storm rolled his eyes. "I will never get used to you calling me that."

WHEN ROSIE DROPPED GLEN off at the office, he kissed her on the top of the head. "Glass of wine, huh?"

"What do you mean?" She batted her eyelashes.

"You knew he was going to be there."

"Oh." She twirled a lock of hair. "Somebody might have mentioned it."

"Manipulative little minx." He patted her ass.

"I may be manipulative, but it's just what you needed."

He smirked. "Good luck tonight."

"Yep. Later." And she was gone.

CHAPTER FIVE

SHARP LEFT

KELLAREAL KNOCKED ON ROSIE'S office door at Hunter Abbey where she was preparing for her dinner talk on 'becoming demon'.

"Come in," she said. When the door opened she was surprised to see Lally on the other side. He normally just appeared wherever. "This is a surprise. Wasn't expecting you."

"There's been a development in the whole kidnapping case. Since your hunters are now demons, Lyric can't legally hold Finngarick's mate. But if she's elemental, she can walk out whenever she wants."

"Sounds right. So why are you telling me this?"

"I can't go get her because, if she's free to walk out on her own, I have no grounds. But if she doesn't know she can walk out on her own, it's a Catch 22. Baby elephants."

"What?"

"You know… The thing about baby elephants."

"No idea how this relates."

"If you chain a baby elephant to a post, it will try and try and try to get free. Once it learns that it won't get free no matter how hard it tries, it's captive forever. They restrain the adults with the same relatively little ankle chain they used when the creature was a baby. As an adult it could easily break away. But it doesn't try."

"Because it believes it can't."

"Precisely."

"So how are we going to get her out now?"

Kellareal shrugged. "We're going to have to get creative."

"Okay. Good. What does that mean?"

"I'm going to ring Lyric's doorbell and ask to see Sheridan O'Malley."

Rosie angled her head. "You think he'd say yes?"

"Beats me. Demons are super unpredictable. So it's worth a try."

"Thanks, Lally. I told Finngarick that, if we don't have her back in two days, I'm going to go get her. One way or another."

"A deadline, is it?" The angel nodded. "I can work with that."

"Glad to hear it. Keep me posted."

He gave an exaggerated salute. "Yes sir! But first."

"First?"

"A question about your Wild Bunch, who it seems were really appropriately nicknamed, since they really *are* a Wild Bunch now. Full-fledged elementals. That idiot scientist could have at least made them angels. The question now is whether they'll use their expanded prowess for Black Swan or not."

"Of course they will."

Kellareal shrugged. "Hope you're right. Power is the ultimate mind fuck."

Rosie grabbed a mason jar out of the screened bookcase behind her. There hadn't been a mason jar there, but she conjured it so smoothly it appeared as if it had been there all along.

"Put a favor in the jar."

"What?"

"A favor. You can't say the word 'fuck'. Angels aren't

allowed."

"That is bullshit."

"Two favors."

"When did you become the language police?"

"I'm not objecting to the language. I'm objecting to *you* using it. Somebody has to rise above. If the rest of us feel free to be common, coarse, or just downright vulgar, that's on us. *You*, on the other hand, have to be the standard bearer."

"Again, that is bu…"

"No. It's not." She shoved the glass jar toward him. "Going for three? I can always use help. Especially now that I'm D.I.T." She took the lid off the jar and waited for him to deposit the favors.

"I want to say bad words like everybody else." He pouted.

She shook her head. "No. Sorry. You can't."

"You don't sound sorry. Why do you get to?"

"Because I don't have wings."

It might not have been logical but it did have a certain kind of sense to it. So, with a sour expression on his otherwise beautiful flawless face, he dropped two little swirling orbs of white light rimmed with yellow into the jar. They hummed and circled like they were on a carousel. Rosie was quick to put the lid on the jar, screw it down tight, and put it back into the screened bookcase.

"Those had better not fall into the hands of…"

"Stop your worrying. They're safe with me. The jar is spelled and won't open for anybody else. Neither will this book cupboard." She stopped and looked over her shoulder. "These don't have to have air or anything. Right?"

He smirked, shook his head, and muttered, "Favors needing air. What next?"

"So let's go get her!"

"Sure. But don't you think you should have a talk with your, um, hunters? They may be wondering what's happening to them."

"You think? How would you like to wake up as a troll? After being an angel for… how long have you been alive?"

"Long time. And your analogy is ridiculous."

"It's not so farfetched. But point taken. I'll stay here and talk to my people. Or demons. You get Sheridan O'Malley and put her back where she belongs."

"Suits me."

He vanished leaving Rosie feeling like that was one enormous item she could safely check off her list.

CHAPTER SIX

BABY ELEPHANTS

S HER LOOKED AT the glass display on the wall where
her bow and arrow were encased.

Lyric followed her gaze. "Strings," he said. "We have
that in common, you and I."

When her head swiveled his direction, he pointed toward the room where he kept his collection of every
imaginable musical instrument. "This, for instance." He
reached for an acoustic guitar that Sher hadn't remem-
bered being there before. "What kind of music do you
like?"

She raised her chin. "I do no' like music."

Lyric laughed and shook his head. His dark hair ruf-
fled with the movement in a most appealing way. "Don't
be childish, Sheridan. It's unattractive."

"I'm no' interested in appearin' attractive to you, demon."

He sighed. "Hmmm. Well, everybody likes music. Perhaps people get different levels of pleasure from music, but everybody likes it."

Sher cocked her head. "Let me tell you what's unattractive. Bein' a know-it-all."

The demon smiled wickedly as the gleam rose in his eyes. His eyes had a sort of inner light that was frightening, captivating, and aggravatingly sexy all at the same time. At times his irises seemed to have little flames that responded to various emotions and danced for the benefit of the observer. Perhaps the flames were a warning. Perhaps they were simply a reflection of interest, mirth, or desire. It was impossible to know. And just as impossible to look away when it was happening.

He pulled the guitar into his lap and began to casually strum a pleasing arpeggio. If Sher had been sleepy, she knew she'd already be yawning and thinking about a nap.

"Would you like to learn to play the guitar, Sher?"

As a matter of fact, she would love to play the guitar, which made it really hard to say, "I can no' stand the sound of that contraption. 'Tis like the squeakin' of old rusty wheels."

Lyric's eyes slanted toward her slowly in a measured way as if testing for the truth of that. "I could teach you easily," he said, ignoring her proclamation of distaste. He just chuckled when she looked the other way.

In looking away from Lyric her eyes had landed on the wall display, which seemed to have been put there to taunt her with her helplessness and captivity. She toyed with the idea that she might be experiencing punishment for being too proud of being selected for D.I.T. For being mate to a beautiful and brave veteran vampire hunter. The folklore she'd heard among the people of Black on Tarry all her life was resplendent with such superstition.

On impulse, without plan or too much thought, she rose, grabbed the guitar out of Lyric's hands and smashed it against the display. The guitar didn't break, but whatever had been the transparent material magically holding the bow aloft vanished. It clattered on the floor as the quiver fell with a soft thud beside it. With a speed and presence of mind she didn't know she had, she picked up the bow, strung an arrow, and whirled around aiming it at Lyric, who was still sitting calmly on the divan.

He got to his feet and raised his hands in a, "Please don't shoot me," pose.

"So you lied after all," Lyric said with more interest than anger. "You *are* a demon. Why play games?"

"I'm no' a demon, eejit. I'm an elf who's ready to go home. Now show me the way or prepare to get stuck and let me warn you these arrows are coated with a juicy little surprise designed especially for creatures such as yourself."

"Sheridan." Lyric lowered his chin and gave her a sobering look. "Only another elemental could break the spell holding your bow."

"Deceiver."

He shrugged. "Sometimes. Not in this case. I wish it wasn't true. I'd like to keep you."

"I'm no' a demon."

He looked pointedly at the wall where the bow had been. "Circumstance says you are."

She bit the inside of her lower lip while contemplating whether or not there could be any truth to that. It was then that she finally pushed her own emotions aside long enough to add up the score. Her unhappiness, missing her mate as she did, worrying about him as she did, had been all she could manage to deal with.

When her reason finally decided to show up for the party, she reviewed the evidence. She hadn't eaten or slept for two weeks. Which was utterly impossible. Unless… If the demon was telling the truth about why she was able to break the bow free, then…

She looked around and, sure enough, her senses told her where there was an active portal that could be used to step into the passes. In her haste to see if she could leave, she forgot all about the homing necklace he'd taken from her. But when she stepped into the passes, she realized she didn't need it. With the other changes, she had, apparently, acquired an internal compass along with incredible speed. She knew exactly how to navigate her way to the D.I.T. house in Dublin. She didn't know how she knew. She just did.

THE HOUSE WAS quiet except for an ancient Swiss clock housed in an elaborately carved German style that stood in the front hall. When it was quiet in the house, the clock noises seemed to grow in volume. Torn glanced toward the front hall and wondered if it would be noticed if he carried the clock over to the commercial trash containers at the end of the next block. He would ever so much more prefer silence to the increasingly irritating tick tock.

He decided that destroying Black Swan property was the sort of thing that could land him back in Marrakesh. Or worse, on floater rotation. So he decided he'd grit his teeth and leave the damnable thing alone.

All the D.I.T. hunters had been called to the Abbey for the briefing. He was curious how the others would take it.

He hadn't really thought there was any chance Sher was coming back to the house in Dublin when he'd asked to stay behind, but he'd maintained a vice grip on the sliver of hope that she'd be more trouble than the creature planned.

Torn didn't have a lot of experience with hope. He'd spent his entire life thinking hope was a silly indulgence practiced by people who'd had such an easy life that they expected, and even believed they deserved, good things. But it only took one instant of holding Sheridan O'Malley in his arms to overhaul his perspective on such things. Occasionally he berated himself for constantly fantasizing that any minute the demon would tire of her and choose to let her go unharmed. But he continued anyway.

WITH PLODDING STEPS, he started up the stairs toward the second floor room he shared with no one, not knowing what he'd do when he got there, wishing he had someplace else, anyplace else, to be. His only reason for going was that the clock noises were a little quieter upstairs, especially if he closed the door and shoved towels against the crack between door and floor.

He was halfway up the stairs when the hairs all over his body began to stand on end. Without any idea what that meant, his intuition informed him that, if it was trouble, he'd rather be downstairs with directional options, than upstairs. Trapped.

HE PAUSED FOR less than a second before reversing direction. Just as his foot hit the old worn and creaky boards of the ground floor, he felt a shift in atmospheric pressure and heard a slight popping sound in the next room. He didn't have to go look to know it was Sheridan.

His mate senses were flooded and filled with her nearby presence.

He opened his mouth to say something, but nothing came out. He told his body to move in that direction, but he was frozen in place. When she turned the corner and saw him standing there, she was visibly filled with the joy and relief that was overwhelming Torn's mind and body.

SHE RUSHED INTO his body, throwing her arms around him and let out a sob followed by a huge gasp of air, almost like she hadn't been able to breathe for weeks. It was odd for her body to be doing things she hadn't actively approved. She hadn't cried since she was a child and had an accident with a fallen tree trunk after being chased by an out-of-sorts badger.

Still unable to make his voice utter a single sound, Torn grabbed onto her like he was alone treading water in the middle of the ocean and she was an inner tube. Sher's sob resolved into quieter expressions of intense relief. He felt the quick intakes of breath that moved her chest against his. Gradually he became aware of wetness where her face was buried in his neck.

"Sher." He breathed her name like a prayer to long forgotten gods. Letting go just long enough to put his hands on both sides of her head, he pulled her face up so that he could get a good look at her. Indeed, the changes in her looks were similar to Shivaun. The freckles he'd loved were gone, replaced with skin that was perfection in the evenness of its color. He immediately decided he loved that just as much. The eyes that had been a warm and welcoming shade of mahogany had become a kaleidoscope of color. Flecks of amber, gold, yellow, and... was that orange?... danced in her eyes, enlivening her irises so that they sparkled with light that seemed to move from within. And he loved that just as much.

He methodically kissed every inch of her face including her eyelids, then kissed each corner of her mouth before pressing his lips to hers. Tongues fought for the privilege of letting the other know how much they were missed and how mightily damn pleased each was to have the other locked in an embrace.

When they parted, Torn managed to rasp, "Are you alright?"

She let out a small laugh full of the satisfaction that came from surviving a situation that could have resulted in death or, in their case, mate separation. Which was worse.

"I am," she said, "now." She looked closely at his face, her gaze flicking from one of his eyes to the other then upward toward his hair. The hint of a frown formed between her brows. "Do you look different?"

He laughed. "Perhaps a bit. You like it?"

She studied him intently looking from one eye to the other before grinning and saying, "Well, aye. I did no' think you could be more beautiful. But perhaps I was wrong." He chuckled as his hands continued to pet her body like he thought that, if he stopped touching, she'd disappear. "Where is everybody?"

"Gone to Scotia. Rosie called the Wild Bunch to the Abbey to talk about, em, things."

"Wild Bunch?"

"That's what everybody in Black Swan started callin' us."

"Oh." It took less than a second to process that and move on. "So we have the house to ourselves?"

Understanding the direction of her thoughts, Torn smiled wickedly. "We do." He began to kiss around the rim of her delicately pointed ear, which triggered an erogenous response. When she squirmed and giggled, he said, "Whate'er should we do with the opportunity?"

"I want to hear what's happened since I've been gone."

"I want to hear everythin' about you."

"But it can wait for ten minutes."

He looked down his nose with sparkling eyes. "I'll ignore that barb, but take the challenge. We'll see if you'll be story tellin' within ten minutes or no'."

Sher turned and went up the stairs so fast that, to human eyes, it would have appeared that she'd vanished. But Torn, having the same newly enhanced abilities, was right behind her reveling in the sheer delight of her laughter and thanking the gods that his good fortune was restored to him.

He filled his hands with athletic curves covered by peaches and cream skin as he backed her toward the two single beds they'd shoved together in the middle of the room when they'd shared quarters.

She raised her arms as he pulled her Henley over her

head and, as he was tossing it aside, he leaned in and sucked her earlobe into his mouth. That elicited a tiny gasp that caused his engorged cock to twitch almost painfully.

"Paddy, Sheridan," he said. "Ne'er leave me again."

She leaned back to look in his eyes, hearing the pain in that simple statement. And she knew in that moment that she'd had the easier lot of it. While she'd spent her time trying to figure out a way home, he was helplessly waiting. Not knowing if she was well or even alive.

"I'll ne'er be away from you by choice. It hurts my heart to know you've suffered."

She removed the rest of her clothing quickly and pulled Torn toward the bed, silently signaling her preference to skip foreplay. She was eager to be joined, to feel him inside her, and it was clear that was what he needed as well.

Pushing his jeans down to his thighs she pulled him back onto the bed, into the cradle of her body, and cried out when he entered her in one mighty thrust. Seated deep, Torn made a sound that could almost be described as a whimper.

Taking charge, as elf females were notoriously fast learners when it came to sex, Sheridan rolled them over, straddled her mate and began to ride him with such ferocity and an abandon so wild, so primitively wanton, that both lost the ability to think. They could only feel the exquisite pleasure of being connected in the most intimate way.

"I can no' hold on with you on top, love," he said. "Feelin' you. Watchin' you. 'Tis too much."

"Let go," she said. "I want you to."

When Sher felt the pulsing spurt of warm liquid, she threw her head back and climaxed in a shudder that almost looked like a seizure. Torn tightened his hands around her waist then abruptly sat up and wrapped his arms around her.

As she slowed, her body seemed to move in the most sensual dance of afterglow and supreme satisfaction. "I missed you, vampire slayer."

They held onto each other, in that position, for a long time, simply grateful to have each other. They needed nothing else. They wanted nothing else.

WHEN KELLAREAL ARRIVED at Lyric's door, he stopped and used the doorknocker, which was an iron figure of a Green Man with an open maw that looked forbidding. Not to him. Of course. But he assumed it was intended to frighten would-be visitors who were less powerful than himself.

He could have entered without knocking, but it would have been so impudent and impolite that news of it would be circulating in elemental circles for centuries. It just wasn't worth it. So he waited.

In a short time Lyric swung the door inward and turned away leaving it standing open, presumably in invitation.

"She's gone," he said with a shrug and who-cares attitude before turning his back, walking back toward his conversation space.

"Gone?" Kellareal repeated.

Lyric turned around. "You getting hard of hearing, old fella?"

The two weren't friends, but both could recognize the other on sight.

Kellareal smirked. "I heard you, demon. I'm just surprised. That's all."

"Why?"

"Well…"

"Has something to do with the fact that she didn't know she's demon when she came here. Right?"

"First, let's be honest. She didn't *come* here. You *grabbed* her out of the passes."

"Tweedle Dee. Tweedle Dum."

Kellareal squinted, shaking his head slightly to indicate confusion. "What!?!"

"I don't like word quibble."

"You mean you don't like to use language with precision?"

Lyric barked out a laugh and flopped down into his cushy divan. "If you're staying, close the door. If not, close the door behind you."

"Why would I be staying?"

"No idea. Yet here you are."

CHAPTER SEVEN

MADE DEMONS

ROSIE WAITED UNTIL EVERYONE was accounted for at the dinner table. Grieve, herself, and fourteen warriors. They were missing only Sheridan O'Malley and Torn Finngarick.

She stood up at the end of the table. "I'd like to ask you if you want the good news or the bad news first, but honestly I don't know if the news is good or bad. Well, there is some good news for sure. You're all *really* good-looking. I mean beyond Abercrombie and Fitch good-looking. We're talking perfect."

The hunters glanced at each other with half-hearted attempts at being surreptitious and said nothing, but silently agreed. They were a right attractive lot.

"The dubious news, and I think most, if not all of you have already figured this out; the serum that originated with Deliverance, intended to allow you to travel the passes for a limited time, has mutated and altered your constitutions. You're no longer elf or human or whatever you were before. You're either demon or you're a damn good imitation."

There was a murmur among the D.I.T. hunters.

"We don't know if this is temporary or permanent. Monq will be looking into it, but he may not be able to tell. Since we don't know, you'll need to continue to keep your homing devices and weapons with you when you're working."

"How does this affect us? Exactly?" Fratmos Dracomb asked from the other end of the long table.

"Fountain of youth, Mo. So long as you're in this state, you're not aging." Another murmur grew in a crescendo of sound, but abruptly died when Rosie began speaking again. "Sounds good on the surface, but if this turns out to be a permanent change, you're going to look the way you look today when your siblings die of old age."

That was met with stunned silence.

"Did they know this could happen? In the lab, I mean?" The question came from Stokes Wyvern, known to teammates as 'Y'. He was a twenty-two-year-old first draft round recruit who was exceptionally talented at, well, everything. The vampire hunting division wanted him, but Rosie got him. Thanks to Simon.

Rosie shook her head. Even though she wasn't a hundred percent sure that Monq hadn't suspected risk, she said, "Was an accident, Y. Pure and simple. No intention here. Now that it's no longer a risk, but a result, the serum will be destroyed along with the formula and the research that went into developing it. You're valued by Black Swan as assets. Yes. But you're also valued as people. This isn't something that would have been allowed if we'd thought there was this possibility.

"You fifteen, possibly sixteen, are the only 'made' demons in existence. And you're all there will ever be."

The hunters looked at each other. It was evident to anyone in the room who was the least sensitive that the air had gone heavy.

"What other changes do we have to look forward to?" Miles Torquezvilla didn't look especially happy about the news so Rosie took the question to be sarcastic.

She sighed and looked at Miles for a few beats. "I don't

believe there will be more physical changes. As to the rest, personality in particular, I hate to ask this, but I'm going to have to request that you keep an eye on each other. We don't anticipate anything, it's just a precaution, because we have no history to draw on. You're a first. And you're unique.

"We're going to spend the night here at the Abbey tonight and tomorrow so that you can get used to the idea and so that we can monitor you as you practice your new abilities. You're no longer confined to your dimension of origin. You can pretty much do anything you want. So, on that note, we can only hope that each of you has a deeply embedded ethical compass. One that is so much part of who you are that it will enable you to rise above the temptations that await. Let character guide your behavior as you prepare to disprove the notion that absolute power corrupts absolutely.

"You *are* powerful now. I hope you're ready to make a commitment to use that to serve the best interest of all worlds, all creatures, everyone everywhere. Because unlike demons, who were designed according to a grand scheme, with a specific guiding purpose, you're free agents."

Again, the hunters silently looked around at each other.

"You've heard that Black Swan peeps are calling you the Wild Bunch?" That got smiles and nods for the first time. "That's all well and good. Let's just make sure they never call us the Crazy Bunch. Or the Evil Bunch."

"We all took an oath to Black Swan, Rosie," Deck said. "It's our first priority and we serve regardless of what form we're in."

The swell of verbal agreement crested then waned.

"I'm hoping none of you ever loses sight of that. A demon's life can be long. Let's make sure your commitment is strong enough to endure if your life turns out to be centuries instead of years. If you use this turn of events well, I'll be your biggest fan. If you don't, I'll be forced to step in. You do not want that to happen."

The room fell silent as a tomb while they contemplated the possibility of living for centuries along with the possibility of being 'corrected' by Rosie. They didn't know exactly how powerful she was, but each suspected she was capable of making good on her threat.

Mo cleared his throat. "Is that, ah, likely? The part

about living for centuries?"

"If this effect proves to be permanent? Yeah. Definitely." Rosie cleared her own throat. "Also, and I'm not doing a unit on sex education, but this needs to be said as a side note for the gentlemen. When it comes to female demons, it's a buyer's market. They're rare and in demand. Only the luckiest males end up with mates of their own kind. Point is, you're going to need to seek out companionship with other species and I'm including people in that. And some, um, adjustments will need to be made regarding, um, technique. Because you're a *lot* more powerful now. And you do not want it said that you loved somebody to death."

A louder murmur rippled through the hunters talking to each other in quiet, but animated ways.

"Questions?"

"Yeah." Everybody turned to look at Blue Winterlast. He was part werewolf like Glen. He was also one of the prize graduates that Rosie had snagged out from under the vampire hunting division. "If female demons are that rare, and we have two…" Everyone turned to look at Shivaun, which immediately brought a rosy blush to her vivid coloring. "Are they going to be spending all their time fighting off the boy demons?" He flicked a glance at Shy before saying, "Is that what happened with Sheridan? Some random demon thought she was an available bachelorette? Is it safe for them to be out running around the passes?"

Rosie's nostrils flared. For a second she wondered if it would be better to let Glen have the too-smart ones. "That's a lot of questions. I'll say this. There's not going to be any elemental party that Shivaun couldn't get an invitation to if she wanted to go." There was cautious laughter because the other hunters weren't sure yet where Rosie was going with that. "She'll be in demand if she wants to be, but nobody is going to take advantage of her. Part of what we're doing here for the next day and a half is schooling all of you up on how to take care of yourselves. *All* of you.

"She's going to be a curiosity out there, but so will you, Blue. If you've retained any werewolf traits, you'll be one of a kind. We won't know how this is going to shake out until we start rattling and rolling. Right?"

"One more question," Blue persisted.

"Sure," Rosie said.

"You said all the lab info on the serum was going to be destroyed."

"Yes. It is."

"What about the weapons that were developed to help us take down demons? They could be used on us."

"That's a good point. I'll have to discuss with Simon whether or not the advantage of having an upper hand is worth the risk of having the technology fall into the wrong hands."

Rosie watched the hunters give each other looks that said they weren't thrilled with the idea. "I'm making an educated guess that there will be a lot of questions tomorrow when you start figuring out how to use your new tool kit. Don't be shy about asking. No matter what it is.

"Alright. Everybody is here except Finngarick and Sher O'Malley. Look around. These people are going to be your closest friends and family for, well, as I said earlier, we don't know how long. But the fact is, they're the only creatures in existence who are like you. Goes without saying that means you share a bond.

"Let's do a little in-the-family experiment." Rosie motioned toward the candelabras that sat end to end running down the center for the entire length of the table. The candelabras were made especially for Black Swan with insignia to specifications. Three candles each. Eight inches high *with* candles. "Reach out and touch the candle flame and tell me how it feels."

Mo laughed. "It's a trick, right? Some kind of trust test?"

Rosie grinned. "If you like."

He shook his head, wiped his hand on his thigh, and passed his index finger through the flame in front of him. As the others watched, his hand returned for a second pass, lingering. He sat back, stared at the flame for a couple of beats, then held his entire palm over it while the others asked questions.

Without moving his hand, he said, "It's warm but in a pleasant way. Not like fire. Like summer sun."

"Not burning?" Rosie said.

He smiled and shook his head again. "No."

The others scrambled to try it themselves. Instead of shoving people out of the way, four went over to the fire and put their hands over the flame there.

Mo looked at Rosie. "What else?" he asked simply.

Rosie was pleased to see that the hunters, at least some of them, were accepting the news with grace and even a sense of adventure. "It's a whole new world, gentlemen. And lady. Meet me out on the field in the morning after breakfast. Eight o'clock. We'll get started." She waved her hand as if to indicate that she was finished, but then turned back. "By the way, I notice that you haven't touched dinner." The hunters still at the table looked down at their plates as if they'd either forgotten food was there or forgotten whether or not they'd eaten. All appeared to be ambivalent. "As a courtesy to the kitchen, let me take a survey. Any of you who actually intend to eat breakfast, raise your hands." When she got no takers on breakfast, she said, "Juice?" Nothing. "Coffee?" Nothing. She turned to Grieve. "Well, there you have it."

AROUND NINE O'CLOCK TORN got a text from Rosie.

Rosie: I'm told your lady is back where she belongs, which means it's time for both of you to get back to work. Meet us at the Abbey tomorrow morning at eight. We're taking the kids on a field trip. Get Sher up to speed and come ready to be teacher's helper.

Torn: Will be there. Tell Shy that Sher is fine.

Since they had no interest in sleeping, the hunters spent the rest of the night discussing their rebirth as demons. Even those who were slower to get their heads around the concept were beginning to fantasize about the possibilities of long lives, if not virtually immortal, and being more powerful in a way that comic book superheroes could only fantasize about.

After the experiment with fire, they decided to try a few others on their own. What began as taps on the biceps escalated to a full-on brawl between Blay McCaul and Tread Phillips. It was an odd spectacle to see two Black Swan hunters laughing while each was doing his best to see if it was possible to inflict damage on the other. They bit, pinched, punched, slapped, kicked, and finally stabbed each other with the knives that hadn't been used to cut meat at dinner.

Still laughing, they fell into big leather chairs.

"That would have come in handy when I was hunting

vampire," Blay said.

Tread nodded. "I'd bet my own life that my partner would still be alive."

"Maybe they'll loan us out."

"Dunno," Tread said. "But I'd do it."

Deck interjected. "We don't know for sure that demons are immune to the vampire virus."

"Yeah," Blay said. "But if…"

LIKE THE HUNTERS hanging out at the Abbey, Torn and Sher had no need for sleep. After several hours of love-making and reveling in the transcendent delight of being reunited, Sher said, "So what 'things' did Rosie call everyone in to discuss? And why are you no' there with them?"

"I asked to stay behind just in case you showed up." He shook his head slightly. "Truthfully, I did no' think there was a chance of that happenin'."

"You must've. Or you would no' have asked to stay."

He smiled and kissed the tip of her nose. "Maybe."

"Do I need to hear what she's talkin' about?"

"Aye. I can catch you up to speed."

When he didn't say anything more immediately, she pressed. "Well?"

"You have no' told me how you came to be here. Or what 'twas like where you were."

After she'd told the entire story with as much detail as she could remember, he said, "You left the necklace behind."

"Aye."

"But you knew how to return here."

"Aye."

"So, you know how the demon kept insistin' that you're like him?"

She answered slowly. "Aye."

"'Tis 'cause ye are."

She stared for a few beats before laughing. "'Tis no' the time for your infamous sense of humor, Finngarick."

"Wish I was jokin' now, love. But 'tis the truth. You said yourself I look different."

"Aye, but…"

"Sher. Search your heart. You know 'tis true."

She took in a deep breath that hitched twice, all the

while staring into his too-blue eyes to make sure she was discerning honesty and not playfulness, but he was right. In her heart she already knew the truth, but wasn't ready to confront it.

"Shivaun?" He nodded. "What does it mean?" she whispered.

"So many things. Things we have no' even thought of yet. *If* 'tis permanent. There's a chance 'tis temporary. Guess we'll have to wait to see. But if 'tis permanent, it means we're goin' to live a long long time. And we're no' gettin' older. It means we can come and go from this world like we were created elemental. Do no' know what all else, but your sister and Deck and I discovered some things on our own…"

"Show me."

"Now?"

"You busy?" she challenged.

It was the middle of the night, but that made no difference in the passes. There was no night and day in the passes. Whether it was midnight or noon at the jump-in point or the final destination, the passes in between were always the same murky gray, lit by some unnamed source that was not the sun.

He grinned, loving her fearless, moxie response to a change that might have thrown a lesser person into a state of stupor.

"Ne'er too busy for a date with my girl. Let's go see what there is to see."

She suppressed a girlish squeal. Barely. "A date? I've heard about dates."

"But you've ne'er been on a date before?"

She narrowed her eyes. "You know I have no'. You just love hearin' that you're the first at… everythin'."

He chuckled. "I do. I really do."

"'Twill be the best date ever. You know why?"

He loved that she sounded a little breathless in anticipation. "Why?"

"'Cause Shivaun and I love nothin' more than exploration. That's why we spent our time away from home growin' up. There was always somethin' new to see in the Forest."

Torn cocked his head and nodded. "Well, in a sense, this is custom made for you. 'Cause I suspect the exploration may be endless."

Grinning she said, "Stop your dawdlin' then."

"I'm no' dawdlin'. I'm appreciatin' my mate's astoundin' beauty."

"Well," she said, "in that case, you can dawdle for a minute."

He laughed, but grew more serious when he pulled her into his arms for a quick standing snuggle. "I can tell you this. We're makin' a change in how we do things. I'm no' goin' first anymore. I'm goin' where you're goin'. No one's goin' to grab you away while I'm no' payin' attention."

"'Tis no' likely. I can find my way back. No matter what."

"If I did no' believe that, we would no' be steppin' into the passes again."

THEY REPEATED THE initial exercise that Torn had done with Deck and Shy. He told her how to let her focus go slightly off so that she could see the misty geysers Rosie called slips.

"They open and close. Sometimes quickly. So we need to be holdin' hands when we go through one of these."

"I have no objection to holdin' hands."

He smiled. "Pick one." She looked around and pointed. "Okay. When you step in, picture the portal underneath St. Patrick's. I'll follow you. Do no' be afraid to go fast. I'll keep up."

She laughed. "Oh. Will ye now?"

"Okay, Sher. Kiddin' aside. Do no' leave me behind."

She smirked. "No' today."

"What I heard was 'not e'er'."

"They say people hear what they want to hear."

"Promise you will no' be separated from me."

She could tell the teasing had turned to anxiety. "Glued to your side, Sir Finngarick."

He smiled. "Holdin' you to that. Give me your hand until we're inside. Then I'll be right behind you."

They stepped in together.

As Torn had instructed, Sher pictured the portal underneath St. Patrick's, just as she had pictured the house in Dublin when she escaped Lyric's lair, and immediately she *knew* how to go.

The passes make up a system of elemental transportation that is a paradox. Like the mechanics of planetary rotation and moon tides, it functions perfectly, never requiring maintenance or repair. Yet according to the current human understanding of physics, it is utterly impossible.

The passes are always in motion. The grid path that lies in front of an elemental traveler constantly adjusts to plot the intended route to reach the destination in the quickest and easiest way.

The trip from the Dublin house to the portal under St. Patrick's was accomplished in four seconds. When they stepped into the stone alcove where the portal could be accessed, Sher said, "That was…"

Torn grinned. "Awesome? Wait till you see this."

He motioned for her to go through the portal.

She stopped dead still on the avenue that lay before her and turned wide eyes to Torn, who laughed. "I know. We had the same reaction."

"Where did all these, em, creatures come from? And why did we no' ever see anyone here before?"

"They were here all along. We could no' see them because they're movin' faster than we were able to see. Truth is this, Sher. Simon's project ne'er would have got off the ground if it was no' for this 'accident' that made us as we are now."

She turned back and 'people' watched for a bit. "Like that sayin'. You have to fight fire with fire." He nodded. "Why are they starin' at us as they go past?"

He shrugged. "No clue. Unless 'tis because we're starin' at them."

They both laughed.

"What did you do next with Declan and Shivaun?"

"We went to see Rosie."

"In America?"

"Aye. New Jersey. We ended up in her bedroom and we got a scoldin' for it. She said there are rules about breakin' in on people's expectations of privacy and I guess she has a point."

"You guess? She was no', um…"

"No. No. She was alone, but no' fully dressed."

"Oh."

Torn chuckled. "Deck was dumb enough to say that he likes lavender lingerie."

Seeing his mate's glare, Torn's mirth quickly dropped away. "I did no' say I like lavender lingerie. And o' course I do no' have any interest in other females underclothin'."

"So you found your way to Rosie's home in New Jersey. Busted in on her. Then what?"

"She confirmed our suspicions."

"That we're demons?"

"Aye."

"Then what?"

"She said she needed to gather all the hunters together for a chat. And she promised me that if you were no' back in two days, she'd go fetch you herself."

"But I was."

"But you were." He smiled. "That's when I begged off goin' to the Abbey."

Sher looked out at the busy promenade. "Can we go explorin'?"

"I want to say aye, but I think we should exercise reasonable caution and hear Rosie's briefin' first. I'm all for adventure, but 'twould no' be smart to set off into the unknown dumb as babies and completely unprepared."

"Stuffy. Stuff. Stuff."

Finngarick blinked at that. "Is that some sort o' weird New Forest expression?"

"'Tis what I'll be callin' you when you leave your bold at home."

"My bold," he repeated drily.

"Aye."

"You are no' accusin' me of cowardice."

She sniffed and looked around before saying, "No' as such."

"NO' AS SUCH!" Torn's eyes blazed in a way that made Sher pull back. She could swear for a second his breath was heated.

"Calm yourself, dragon. I would ne'er make such a suggestion. I'm just sayin' 'twould do no harm to take a peek inside one of those doors."

Torn shook his head. "Be mad if you want, but no. There's no fun in adventure when it ends without survivin' to tell the tale. Do you grasp what I'm tellin' ye?"

Sheridan, who was much less experienced in the world than Finngarick, slowly began to recognize the wisdom of that. "You're sayin' the worst that could happen in the New Forest is bein' chased by a ragged-tooth bear. And the passes are uncharted jeopardy."

Torn began to relax, seeing that she would accept reason. "Exactly. I like that you're a thrill seeker. But there's a fuck all difference between bravery and foolhardiness." He ran a hand through his hair searching for the right thing to say. He didn't want to discourage her sense of adventure. And he didn't want to leave the impression that he was a pussy either. When he looked up, one particularly curious demon had slowed down. He'd given Sheridan the once-over, then did it twice and was going for three times. "What the fuck are you lookin' at?"

The demon smirked, looked at Sher again, then decided to move on.

Finngarick took in a deep breath. He wasn't used to explaining his behavior. In fact, heretofore, he'd mostly had a firm policy against it. But that was *before*.

"Havin' a hard time tryin' to find the right way to say this."

"Why?" Sher's expression softened. "'Tis just me. Anythin' can be said 'tween you and me."

He nodded. "Before you, I would no' have hesitated, because I just did no' care. For the first time in my life I have somethin' to live for. And I plan to be livin' and enjoyin' it for a very long time." He pushed her very red hair away from her neck and traced her ear with his thumb.

"You got another way to thrill me?"

His smile widened into a grin made all the more salacious by his impossibly white, impossibly perfect teeth. He stepped in so close that their bodies were touching. She inhaled the seductive scent of demon musk and, for a minute, thought she might be a little dizzy with buzz. That was new.

"I'd *thrill* you right here against this wall that might or might not be stone in the middle of where'er, whate'er, this is if 'twould no' draw a crowd. But everybody seems far too interested in you. And that makes me nervous as a cat."

He pulled her into a kiss that began as playful, but turned steamy in seconds. When he smelled the scent of her arousal, he said, "Let's get out of here. Nothin' in the passes could compare to bein' *alone* with you."

She pulled away giggling, then before he knew what was happening, stepped around and jumped on his back. "Give me a ride."

He hooked his forearms behind her knees so that she

would be secure for a piggyback ride to break *all* previous records. They traveled straight back to the Dublin house, bypassing the portal, making use of Finngarick's newly acquired strength and speed that were impressive even by demon standards.

AT EIGHT O'CLOCK the following morning Torn and Sher appeared in the great hall out of thin air. The hunters gathered there did not gasp or shriek, which was the typical human response to people suddenly appearing out of thin air. Instead, they seemed to take it in stride and acted as natural about it as if they'd been demons for ages.

The one exception was Shy, who put on an excited burst of speed to rush her sister and attack her with a big squeeze of a bear hug. "Was so worried," Shivaun said. "Did that thing hurt you?"

Sher shook her head. "No' at all. He wanted to teach me guitar."

"What?" Shy blinked.

"Aye. He's a music demon, I guess. Claimed that he could make me fall in love if he sang to me. But he has compunctions. He said he would no' do that because it would no' be real. Or somethin' like that."

"Oh. Well. So you ne'er felt like you were in danger?"

Everyone had drawn close and was gathered round to overhear the conversation by that point.

"No. I ne'er felt like he meant to harm me. Just keep me. And, o' course, I did no' want to stay. So we argued about that. Constantly. And food. We argued about food because I was no' havin' any. He said either I was a demon or I needed to eat. I guess he was right about that. I had the feelin' that he enjoyed the arguin'. Maybe he's lonely?"

"Hmmm. Could he no' seek out others like himself?"

"Aye. I suppose."

"So how did you get away?"

"He'd put my bow on his wall in a case that looked like glass. I guess it was some kind of magic spell. He was sittin' there playin' his guitar like everythin' was fine. No' like he was holdin' someone against her will. And all of a sudden the whole thing made me mad. I grabbed his guitar out of his stupid hands thinkin' that I did no' want to hear that anymore. I smashed it against the case thing on the wall. The guitar did no' break, but the case disappeared. I picked up my bow and threatened him.

"But when I did that, I could see the way out. It was strange. I was askin' myself why I had no' seen the way out before. He had my necklace, but when I stepped into the passes, I found I did no' need it. I just *knew* the way back to the house in Dublin."

She stopped and smiled at Torn, only then realizing that she'd drawn a small crowd that was enraptured by her tale of escape. Not being used to public speaking, she immediately became shy.

Rosie, who'd caught most of the story standing back at a distance, said, "You see? The O'Malleys can take care of themselves."

One by one the hunters welcomed Sher back.

"You sure he's not coming after her?" Blue asked Rosie.

"I'm not sure about that," Rosie replied. "But by the end of the day, I'm going to feel pretty good about Sher and Shy being equipped to handle whatever jumps up."

The twins looked at each other and had a silent dialogue that only the two of them were privy to. After another brief hug, Sheridan turned to take Torn's hand

and interlaced her fingers with his.

"Let's get started," Rosie said.

THEY BEGAN BY DISCUSSING the difference between slips and portals.

"Come on. We're gonna take a field trip. Buddy system. Your partners are your buddies.

"We're going to Edinburgh via a slip. Then we're going to access one of the portals under the Walter Scott Monument. Stay close. If we get separated, come back here. If you didn't want dinner or breakfast or juice or coffee, you won't need your necklaces today. But I want you to be in the habit of having them with you. Everybody got your homing device?"

They all nodded assent.

"Save your questions. When we get to the portal at Edinburgh, we'll stop and talk."

THE HUNTERS DIDN'T bother to feign sophistication. They gaped openly when the portal opened into a busy elemental thoroughfare.

"Where did all these…?" Rosie heard one of the hunters begin to ask.

She smiled. "Elementals. There are angels, demons, sylphs, gnomes, and, well, you know the list." They didn't necessarily know that list, but she continued anyway. "When we were figuring out how you were going to chase down intruders, I guess I overlooked the limitations in your internal gauge calibrations. Elementals' vibrations adjust to circumstances and environment automatically. You couldn't see the activity because they were moving faster, too fast for you to follow physically or visually. Like I said, this is a shakedown cruise. We're figuring it out one mistake at a time."

"Real encouraging," Blue muttered to his partner.

Rosie looked at Blue. "I hope the biggest hurdles are behind us. But if not, we're in it together. Wish I could tell you something more conclusive."

"Hey," Mo said. "We're pioneers. And eternal youth isn't all bad. Preserving this fabulous form forever is worth a couple of hiccups." When he struck a couple of body-builder poses, his partner shoved him so that he lost his balance.

"Seriously," Deck leaned toward Finngarick, "the curiosity seems to be focused on our partners."

Torn's keen awareness had come to the same conclusion. "I know. We'll talk to Rosie about it later."

Deck nodded.

"Okay." Rosie clapped her hands. "Here's your first assignment. Go to your elementary school library." While she talked she handed out hundred dollar bills. One to each hunter. "Take a book, but leave a hundred dollars with the librarian. Since you're staying with your partners, that will be two library stops each. And this is important, so listen up. Do it without causing a stir.

"Just before you step into Loti Dimension, you'll have an opaque view into the world you're about to enter. Like a thin veil between you and the destination. Check and make sure you're not going to surprise anybody. If you are, move around until you find a secluded spot. Or moment."

She looked at her watch. "Meet back at the Abbey in two hours. Anybody want lunch today?" Everybody shook their heads. "Alright. Consider this a bonding exercise with your partners. You'll get to figure out traveling like demons and see where your partner went to school as a child. Win. Win."

"Questions?"

"Yeah," Blue said. "Are we likely to encounter any other, ah, elementals who'd want to interact with us?"

"In a confrontational way?"

"Well, that, or even, 'Hey. Haven't seen you around. What kind of demon are you?' sort of way."

She pursed her lips. "That's a probability. I don't have a count. I'm not sure anybody does. But if I had to guess, I'd say that there are no more than a thousand elementals altogether. Not so many that everybody doesn't know everybody else, at least on sight if not personally. New demons don't happen very often. Sixteen new demons is a veritable population explosion that's bound to cause a ripple.

"Like people, some are more outgoing, more social, than others. If you're approached by other elementals who want to know who you are and what kind of demon you are, just say, 'I'm a newbie. I work for Rosie Storm and I'm on a time-sensitive errand. Catch up later?' and keep moving.

"If your change turns out to be permanent, eventually you're going to know everybody. Annnnnnd what they're up to. That's going to make your D.I.T. job a piece of cake. Word will get around that Loti Dimension is patrolled by sixteen demons who are serious about keeping the mischief confined to the natives."

"So everybody knows you?" Asked by Bailey Cruz, one of the young recruits that Rosie stole from the vampire hunters.

"They do." She nodded. "Because my genetic makeup is more or less, um, unique."

"What if they speak a different language?" Bailey asked, growing either bolder or more curious.

Rosie snapped her fingers and hit her head with the heel of her hand. "Forgot about that. You can speak every language."

The hunters looked shocked.

Finally Shivaun cleared her throat and said, "*Every* language?"

"Yeah," Rosie nodded. "Every language in Loti Dimension and every language in every dimension."

Mo looked at his partner and grinned. "That's a good

trick."

"Indeed it is," Rosie said. "Use it wisely. Those of you who were vampire hunters, remember you're not just warriors anymore. Now you're diplomats first."

THE NORTHERN IRISH VILLAGE of Dunkilly had a single campus for primary and secondary education and it didn't look particularly well-funded. Sher had sensed Finngarick tense when Rosie had said to collect a souvenir from childhood. She said nothing about it, but resolved to make sure he knew he was supported.

School was closed when they arrived. So being seen wasn't an issue. Neither was the fact that the lights were out, because they discovered that, among other amazing enhancements, they could see in near-dark conditions.

"What book would you like to get?" Sher asked.

"Does it matter?" She shook her head. "Well, then." Without taking his eyes away from her, he reached out to the stack standing on his right and withdrew a book. He handed it to Sher and smiled. "What did I choose?"

She looked down at the book cover. "*Cú Chulainn.*

Suits you."

Torn cocked his head. "Suits me?"

She beamed. "A great Irish legend. Like you."

His first reaction was to accuse her of joking, but he could tell by reading her energy that she was not. She actually believed him to be special. And the knowledge of that almost knocked the wind out of him. Torn had known he'd been mightily blessed the day he realized Sheridan O'Malley was his mate, but he'd never expected to be compared to a great hero, admired on such a grand scale by anyone.

He couldn't prove that he was a few inches taller, but he felt a few inches taller.

"Sher. I'm no'…"

She pressed two fingers to his lips to shush him. "You're far more than you give yourself credit for. And I can prove it."

Torn chuckled. "How can you prove it?"

"Where's the pub?"

He smirked. "What makes ye think there's a pub?"

"My tutor told me. There's a pub in every village."

"Well, she'd be right. Why do ye want to go there? I

fear you'll find that people do no' think as much of me as you do. And I'm no' sure I want you to see that."

"Trust me. I know what I'm doin'."

"Very well. I find that I have a very hard time sayin' no to you."

She laughed and took his hand. "Old school. Let's walk."

"Whatever you say."

It was an easy ten minute walk to the pub in the late afternoon. The work day had ended for most people, but it was still light out. They passed a few people on their way who stared unabashedly. Some looked confused, like they were trying to remember how they knew Torn, but couldn't place it.

The pub was noisy, smoky, and crowded.

"Show me a peer."

"A peer?"

"Somebody close to your age."

Torn looked around for a minute and then pointed to a man standing at the bar.

"What's his name?"

"Arlan."

"Who was he to you?"

Torn shrugged, but Sheridan's mate sense read the pain he was covering up.

"Just another kid who made me want to be someplace else," he said.

"Was he liked by the others?"

"Liked?" He smiled ruefully. "Oh, aye. He was thought to be the sauce by young and old alike."

"And that means…"

Torn glanced away. "Golden lad. Ringleader. Respected family."

"Very well. Come on."

She started toward the bar where Arlan was hunched over a pint.

"Wait!" Finngarick grabbed her and pulled her close enough so that he could talk into her ear and only she could hear. "I'm no' lookin' for a reunion with," he glanced toward the bar, "that fucker."

Sher's eyes danced. "Well, you can no' always get what you want. I sense you're havin' a hard time trustin' me and that can no' be helped. But you will come with me like it or no'."

Torn pulled away and set his jaw, trying to decide whether he was going to let her have her way or not. "Since it seems all fired important to ye, I'm goin' along with ye this time. But do no' make a habit of tellin' me what I will or will no' be doin'."

Sher smiled, batted her lashes, and got on her toes to give him a quick kiss on the cheek. "Understood."

Arlan was leaning against the old worn bar with both elbows when Sher approached on his left side.

"Arlan?" she asked brightly.

He turned his head toward her. "Do I know you?" His gaze flicked to Torn standing behind her, slightly off to the side. As Arlan's gray eyes traveled over Torn, Sher thought she saw a flicker of recognition.

"I'm Sheridan O'Malley. My mate and I are in town for a few minutes and I asked to stop into the pub. He grew up here. Torrent Finngarick? You remember him?"

Arlan looked past Sher again. "Finngarick?" He ran a hand over a day's growth of bristle on his weathered face. Sher couldn't help thinking he looked so much older than Torn. "Aye. You look, em, different," he said to Torn.

"I am different," Torn supplied.

Sher cast a warning look his way and he shrugged.

"Let us buy you, em," she looked at the special of the day, "a cod and cabbage supper. Maybe another pint." He looked down at the pint he was working. She pointed to a snug in the corner. "We could sit over there. Catch up a bit durin' the short time we're here?"

Arlan looked at Torn again and took a sip from his mug before saying, "I might do with supper and another pint."

"Very nice of you," Sher said. "Let's grab the table before somebody else gets it."

Arlan snorted at that. Sher supposed that meant the pub wasn't expecting a big crowd for dinner. She told the bartender to bring over one supper and three pints then waved for Arlan to lead the way.

Torn held her back when she started to walk after Arlan. "We do no' have any money." He raised a well-shaped eyebrow.

After pursing her lips in thought, she said, "I'll go to the 'ladies' and get some," she offered. Torn shook his head for several beats before nodding. For an odd combination of gestures, he made himself clear.

When they were seated, Sher turned to Arlan. "So what have you been doin' since school?"

"Fishin' with my da. And my grandda on days when he's up to it."

"That's nice. A family business. Bet it's excitin'." Arlan looked at Sher like she must have escaped the looney bin. "Is that what you always wanted to do?"

Arlan shrugged and looked around the room. "Suppose." It was evident that Arlan had never thought about what he might want to do. And there was a good chance no one had ever asked him that question before.

"Well, what else have you been up to? Done much travelin'?"

He glanced at Torn then looked at Sher. "Went to Derry once."

"That's an adventure."

"Oh, aye, 'twas."

Sher waited for him to continue. When he didn't, she said, "Soooooo. What do you do for fun around here?"

"I do no' spend a lot of time contemplatin' fun. I work. I have my pint and my supper. I go home. One day becomes another."

"Well, no matter. You'll always be better than Finngarick here. Right? At least there's that."

A little light came into Arlan's eyes. He looked at Torn. "Aye. There's that."

Sher sighed then elbowed Torn. "I need to run to the ladies'," she said pointedly.

He let her out, sat back down, and passed time silently with a man who'd helped make his childhood a bitter memory.

Just before Sher returned, Arlan said, "Somethin' wrong with your pint?"

Torn looked from Arlan to the mug in front of him then back to Arlan. "Aye. Like everythin' else in this town, it blows."

Sher appeared before Arlan could think of an answer. She placed Irish pound notes on the table and said, "Arlan. 'Twas so nice to meet you. Sorry we have to go, but time's up. Enjoy your supper." She smiled. "And your life. Such as it is."

Outside in the street in front of the pub, Torn said, "What in Paddy's name was that about, Sher? He'll always be better than I?"

It was dark and the evening air was chilly in the North Sea town of Dunkilly, but Torn and Sher were no longer susceptible to discomfort because of weather. Nor did they have any trouble seeing each other's faces as if it was light of day.

Sher cocked her head. "Do you no' get it, love?"

Torn's brows came together and tiny lines formed, but they were temporary because he was beyond the vagaries of wrinkles. "Get what?"

"Arlan is just a small samplin' of the town that did you wrong, the first one we happened on. We would find a similar story amongst the others if we had time and inclination to pursue it. The fact is that Arlan works on the family fishin' boat every day then hunches over a pint alone at night. He's ne'er been more than two hours away from home. He's ne'er done a single thing that would make a lastin' impression on the world.

"You, on the other hand, have been all over the world as a human and across dimensions as a demon. You've battled the monsters that people like Arlan do no' even know exist and done your part to keep the world's residents safe at night. Done so many things. Seen so many things." She grinned. "And ye have me."

As Sher had talked Torn felt his chest swelling with self-esteem and gratitude. She was a hundred percent right. He'd gladly live through every minute of his life again if it would bring him to that exact moment when he stood on the street outside the pub in Dunkilly looking into the face of the most precious treasure imaginable.

He didn't trust himself to speak, but showed her how he felt by pulling her into a kiss so fervently felt, long, sweet, deep.

"'Tis your turn. Did you go to a school with a library?"

She laughed and shook her head. "We had a school and the school had books. No library as such, but it'll do."

"I can no' wait for you to show me your home."

"You'll love it."

He nodded, cupped her face with his hands and ran a thumb over her cheek, just for the pleasure of touching and marveling at what a wonder she was. "I know I will."

ALL THE HUNTERS made it back to the Abbey with a show-and-tell souvenir except for one hunter who found a convenience store in the location where his elementary school had been.

"That's a valuable lesson," Rosie told the group. "Razz, what did you picture when you traveled through the passes to get to your elementary school?"

"The school," he replied.

"But when you arrived it wasn't there." He nodded. "So your internal navigation system led you to the location where it had been. I don't know that you'll ever need that tidbit, but if it turns out that you're perma-demons, at some point you might need to know that's how it works.

"Anybody hungry yet?" They shook their heads. "Sleepy? Thirsty?"

"Horny," said Mo.

Rosie laughed. "That doesn't go away. As long as you're not feeling any of the other physical drives, it's safe to say you can travel like a born elemental. But if you ever feel the slightest craving, put yourself on the D.L. until we sort you out.

"Although, an occasional desire to eat may not mean you're reverting. Some demons may go for hundreds of years without eating and then suddenly have an inexplicable desire for, say, meatloaf."

Torn shook his head. "If you say so."

Rosie chuckled. "Or whatever. Next we're going to talk about other environments. As you know, when you went through training as people, you were told never to chase a target into another dimension. You were cleared to go into the passes, but not beyond.

"Now you're going to be cleared to go anywhere, but we need to work up to it. There are a lot of other realities out there and some of them will seem, well, surprising? I believe you've gone through a total transformation. You don't just have demon bodies. I think you have demon minds as well. If I'm right about that, new environments won't be frightening, alarming, or disturbing. It won't seem more unusual to you than traveling to the Amazon rain forest or the Grand Canyon or the Tunisian desert. These places are vastly different, but you take the change of landscape or weather or culture in stride.

"I think that's the way you will view the new experiences that will unfold for you, when you begin interdimensional travel. Whether I'm with you or not, anytime you feel threatened, launch yourself into the nearest slip and think about home.

"For the next hour or so my friend, Kellareal, who is an angel, is going to talk to you about the general comportment expected of you now that you've joined the community of worldwalkers. After that, we're going to go exploring."

Sher looked at Torn and grinned. He shared her smile, loving that the idea of new experiences delighted her so much.

THAT EVENING SIXTEEN HUNTERS saw things they couldn't have imagined were possible. They petted dragons with shiny scales of emerald green and cobalt blue. They walked over lava fields without harm in a world with an orange sky. They stood on a windy plateau and watched a battle between Vikings and Angles in a world that was twelve hundred years behind Loti Dimension.

Every new experience was more stunning than the last.

When she believed they'd had a sufficient sampler of life as a demon, she said, "Meet me back at the Abbey," and disappeared.

When the hunters, all sixteen, returned feeling powerful and powerfully pleased with themselves, they found the dining table and chairs had been replaced with comfortable lounge furniture.

"Take a seat," Rosie told them. "Congratulations. You passed the test. If you could find your way home from Breitlingen Dimension, you can get back here from anywhere. Consider yourselves certified.

"Now. About today. Thoughts?"

The hunters looked around at each other.

Deck was first to speak. "I understand why you have a concern about how we use this, ah, ability. Being able to do anything is…"

"Let's fill in the blank. Seductive? Tempting? Overwhelming? Dizzying? Mind blowing?"

The last choice made a few of them chuckle.

"Aye," Shivaun said. "All of that."

Rosie turned to her. "I'm sure it makes adapting to the world outside the New Forest seem easier."

Shivaun nodded. "Do we, em, Sheridan and I have any special concerns?"

Rosie cocked her head. "What do you mean?" The question was reflex, but before Shy could answer, Rosie took her meaning. "Oh!" She shook her head vigorously. "You can't be forced to do anything you don't want to do by another elemental. And the males are not stronger than you. As I said earlier though, you, as a single female demon, can be the belle of the ball if you want."

Shy raised her chin like she was thinking that over.

Rosie went on. "I'm thinking that Black Swan doesn't need to support the expense of maintaining residences. You can work your districts from here as easily as any-where. So I'm recalling all of you to the Abbey. From now on it will be home base and also home if you want. Of course, if you want to maintain a separate place, on your own farthing, be my guest. I'd just ask that your main residence be here in Loti Dimension." At that several of the hunters grinned at each other as if to say, 'Life is strange'. "Move your stuff back here today." Almost to herself, she said. "I guess we can let the kitchen staff go.

"Other thoughts?"

"If we don't need to sleep and don't need rest," Razz said, "are we supposed to work all the time?"

"No. Of course not. You still need free time just like before. Only now you've got a much broader range of choices on how you'll spend it."

Torn leaned into Sher and whispered in her ear, "Got unlimited ways to thrill my girl."

Sher gave him a smile that said she was imagining couplings with a gorgeous redheaded demon in a hundred different ways in a hundred different worlds and she found that, as a demon, her imagination had expanded to keep pace with her newly acquired worldwalker abilities.

CHAPTER EIGHT

SHIVAUN

THE TWINS AND their partners arrived at the Dublin house to gather their things and clear out their belongings. They were standing in the kitchen, taking one last look around when Lyric appeared behind Sheridan. When she turned around, he was there in all his captivating glory.

She grabbed Deck's light gun and pointed it at Lyric.

The demon put his hands up. "I come bearing gifts." When he opened his palm, the homing device necklace fell so that it was dangling from the cord looped around his thumb.

"I'm no' goin' with ye, demon," Sheridan spat at Lyric as she put both hands on the pistol to steady it in the most deadly way.

"I'm not here for you, Sheridan. Just returning your,

ah, device," said Lyric.

Torn had sprung to an instant alert and was in between Sher and Lyric. "Is this the fucker who took ye?" He felt for his pistol, but wasn't wearing it. Which was a good thing because he surely would have stunned the demon into a permanent state of stupor if he could have.

"No offense." Lyric looked at Sher calmly. "I enjoyed my time with you very much."

Torn started toward Lyric, but Deck grabbed hold of him. "Easy, brother. Let's decide how to handle this together."

Lyric never took his eyes away from Sher, as if Torn was of no concern. That, of course, infuriated Torn even more. Lyric continued, "But I'm not here for you."

To everyone's surprise, Shivaun stepped between Lyric and Sher and pressed Sher's arms down so that the gun was aimed at the floor.

"Let's hear what the beautiful creature has to say."

All three of her teammates' heads jerked toward Shivaun when they heard her call Lyric a 'beautiful creature'.

Sher gaped. "Shivaun. What are ye doin'? This is the

demon who took me."

"I know." She shrugged. "But he did no' harm you. And maybe he had a good reason."

At that Lyric gave Shivaun a blindingly brilliant, ear to ear, closed mouth smile.

Sher's mouth fell open even wider. "A good reason? Are you ill?"

Shivaun glanced back at Sheridan. "No," she replied as if it was a serious inquiry into her health.

Sher looked at Torn. "What's happened to my sister while I..." she glared at Lyric, "was being HELD AGAINST MY WILL?!?"

Torn replied as if it was a serious question. "She's missed you. Terribly much. She's worked. And worked. And she's told me stories of the two of you growin' up in a strange land where time stood still."

Sher looked at Torn like she was having a hard time processing his response. "Has everybody here taken a literal pill?" Torn frowned slightly. "That does no' explain this strange behavior."

"No. It does no'." He shrugged his powerful shoulders. "Maybe she's attracted to him."

Truthfully, Torn didn't care who was attracted to who so long as none of the parties were Sheridan O'Malley.

Sher looked stupefied. Then horrified. Then stupefied. "Likes him! She can no' *like* him. He's a kidnapper."

"But he did no' harm you," Shivaun repeated softly.

Sher acknowledged that Lyric hadn't harmed her per se, but captivity shouldn't be looked upon with nonchalance either.

"He held me against my will," Sher repeated with clenched jaw, glaring at the demon past Shivaun's shoulder.

"I offered to trade her for you," Lyric said to Shivaun.

Surprised by that revelation, Shivaun turned toward Lyric and cocked her head with wide eyes. "You did?" He nodded as his attention drifted down to her lips and lingered there. "Why?"

"She's mated. You're not," he said casually. Then he raised his eyes and locked gazes with her. "But there's also your name. Shivaun is a name I could say thousands of times without tiring. On my errands. In my sleep." He deliberately let his voice drop an octave and leaned into her slightly. "Making love."

Shivaun shuddered visibly. It made Lyric smile and brought the dancing firelight into his eyes.

"Oh for…" Deck said. "Rosie said we could understand all languages. That goes for bullshit, too."

"But she said no," Shy said.

"Yes. She thought she was protecting you. I suppose she thought being traded to me was a nightmare."

"Would it be?" Shivaun said, looking all the more interested in what Lyric had to say.

"Shy!" Deck stepped forward and gently moved Shivaun out of the way. "Are you bewitching her?"

"Not a witch, boy," Lyric said.

"Bespelling? Enchanting? I don't care what you call it. Whatever you're doing, stop it, unless you want to be the first field guinea pig for what happens when we cast the blue net over a demon."

Lyric narrowed his eyes. "I'd be careful if I were you. What works on me probably works on you as well." The demon raised his eyebrows and waited to see what else Declan had to say.

While Deck was thinking that Lyric was smarter than he'd hoped, Torn spoke up. "You're thinkin' like a human,

Deck. We do no' need weapons to stop this creature in his tracks."

Deck's eyes slid slowly to Lyric. "I guess that's right."

"Nobody is bespellin' anybody," Shivaun said. "I just happen to think he has a certain… appeal."

"He's a DEMON, *Shy*!" Sheridan had not gotten used to people calling her sister Shy and almost made it sound like a pejorative.

"So are YOU, *Sher*!" Shivaun threw the biting inflection right back at her twin.

Torn, Deck, and Lyric watched in fascination as the twins perfectly synchronized crossing their arms as if they were two people and one brain. The only difference was that one held a gun-shaped object while the other did not.

They glared at each other wordlessly for a few seconds before Sheridan said, "Fine! Just wait 'til you see his cave. He does no' have a single window."

Shivaun blinked. "I have no' said anythin' about seein' where he lives. I'm just sayin' we should let the, um, creature speak. Hear him out. Our da would demand it."

Sheridan gave her head a quick jerk to the left and resumed gaping. "Our da would take a pitchfork to my kidnapper! No' insist on treatin' him like a guest."

Shivaun turned to Lyric. "She might have a point, demon. What have ye to say for yourself?"

Lyric looked at Shivaun like she was something marvelous to eat. "Do I have permission to lower my hands?"

Shivaun waved impatiently and said, "Tell your story, but be warned. If we do no' care for it, my partner will stun you into statue land."

The colorful description caused Torn to tear his glare away from Lyric long enough to exchange a glance with Deck.

Lyric directed his focus to Shivaun and spoke to her as if no one else was there.

"I was on an errand when I passed by a troupe of four travelers in the passes. It piqued my curiosity for three reasons. First, because travelers don't usually move about in groups. Second, they were moving so slow they were practically standing still. And third, I sensed something quite impossible. Or so I thought. A female demon. A prize beyond all others."

He noted with considerable satisfaction that Shivaun was drawn into his story like he was telling a spell-laced tale.

"In all of creation I know of only three. Two of them are mated to gods. The other, let's just say she's preoccupied and not interested in being courted."

"Courted." Shivaun repeated the word as though it was a paradise-like vacation destination.

"Yes." Lyric leaned in.

Deck pulled his pistol. "Step back." Lyric raised both eyebrows, but did as Declan requested. "You can talk, but not move."

Lyric cast a look at Declan that gave away nothing then turned his attention back to Shivaun.

"So when I realized that I had passed within inches of a miracle, I turned back. I could see that they were taking her for granted, not taking care with her as they should. So I took her hand and gave a little tug." He smiled his blindingly beautiful smile. "And she came with me. Since demons can't be forced to do what they don't want to do, I was ecstatic. I couldn't believe my good fortune. The she demon was choosing to come home with me.

"But when we arrived, she was not at all what I expected. I thought she was playing a game I didn't understand when she claimed to have been abducted. I thought she wanted to live out some version of a 'capture' fantasy. So I went along to see what would happen. Then she claimed to be elf and not demon. She said she needed a toilet. So I built her a toilet to shame all palaces and she never used it. I brought her food and drink, but she never touched it. She also never slept, but still claimed she was not one of us.

"I couldn't force her to tell the truth until she was ready. So I decided to bide my time and try to convince her that, if she was looking for a mate, she should consider me." He lowered his voice, his gaze boring into Shivaun's. "I have a lot to offer."

"So you really didn't think you were kidnapping her?" Shivaun asked.

"Shy!" Deck said. "Please tell me you are *not* buying this load of demon droppings."

Shivaun glanced over her shoulder. "Seems plausible to me." Lyric smiled like the Cheshire cat. "Is that all?"

"Oh, no," Lyric purred. "There's more."

"Well, what is it?"

"I'd like to spend time with you." His eyes flicked to

Torn, Sher, and Deck just before he said, "*Alone.*"

"Why?" Shivaun breathed.

"I'll get to know you better. You get to know me better."

"You're talking about a date!" Sher spat. "You want to date my sister, you conniving creature."

He ignored the last half of what Sher said. "Yes! A date! I, Lyric, want to go on a date with you, Shivaun." Shy closed her eyes briefly from the pure pleasure of the way the demon said her name. "What could be bad about that?"

"What could be bad about that," Sher began, "is that you might just decide to keep her. You made it clear to me, when you believed I couldn't get away, that you had no intention of letting me go."

Lyric did his best to look innocent. "I'm sorry if I gave you that impression."

"Why you…" Sher started toward Lyric, but Shy held out a stiff arm that stopped her progress.

"Just a minute," Shy said. "'Tis my choice."

"Shivaun," Sher said. "Do no' be taken in by this thing. I know he's beautiful…"

"Hold on," said Torn indignantly.

Sheridan continued without missing a beat, "But he's no' what he appears to be at the moment."

Shivaun turned to Sher. "Rosie said we're no' in danger."

"That's because she does no' know this demon."

"I get that you're worried. I felt the same way when you took up with Torrent Finngarick."

"I didn't 'take up' with Torn. We're *mated*!"

"Still."

"Still? What can I say to get you to see reason?"

"I'll go along with that," Deck said.

"Look." Shy put a hand to her forehead for a second. "I'm no' proposin' a handfastin'. I'm considerin' a date."

"And you do no' see a problem there?"

"No. What's the problem?"

Sher crossed her arms. "The problem is this. How many dates have you been on?"

Shy would have flushed if she was still elf. As it was she simply looked flustered. "None."

"That's right. You have no, as in zero, experience with the opposite sex." Lyric's head slowly swiveled to Shivaun and it was clear that she just became his entire raison d'être.

"So?" Shivaun crossed her own arms and adopted a stance that looked like she was preparing to dig into an intractable position.

"So!" Sher turned to Lyric. "How old are you again?"

Lyric dropped his chin, but kept his eyes on Sher. "Very."

"Right. And how many females have you 'dated'?" She put that in air quotes. "Do no' bother to lie. We will *all* know if you do."

"Many," he gritted out grudgingly.

To Shivaun, she said, "Exactly. Your first experience with the opposite sex should no' be with someone who…"

"Knows what he's doing?" Lyric offered.

Shivaun gave Lyric a coy smile like she understood that to be a sexual reference.

"Someday you may be lucky enough to be mated," Sher went on.

"And if that happens," Shy said, "it won't hurt anythin' for me to have a broader understandin' of… things. From what I hear, your mate had the broadest 'understandin' possible." She put 'understanding' in air quotes.

Sheridan gaped.

Torn said, "Let's just…"

"Wait a minute," Deck said to Torn. "A catfight between the twins could be kind of, I don't know, fun."

Torn glared at Declan. "'Tis my mate you're talkin' about."

"Yes. But it's my fantasy you're trying to deprive me of."

"Shut the fuck up," Sheridan told Deck. "Nobody is fightin' anybody. If my sister will no' see reason and wants to make an epic mistake with this dick of a demon, then so be it."

"'Tis my life," Shivaun said, as haughty as any teenager.

"Indeed 'tis," Sher confirmed. "So go on. Be off with ye."

"We're supposed to be moving our stuff to Hunter Abbey. Or has everybody lost sight of that fact along with their minds?" Deck asked.

"You're implyin' that we've lost *our* minds?" Torn asked incredulously. "Thirty seconds ago you were promotin' a catfight fantasy between my mate and her sister."

"I was joking," Deck said.

Torn shook his head. "Do no' think so."

"Well, I didn't think it was going to happen which is the same thing as joking."

Torn narrowed his eyes. "That sounded suspiciously like the demon double speak that we keep hearin' about."

Lyric interjected. "Double speak is just a rumor without basis in fact."

Torn looked at Lyric. "Right. Fake news."

"No, really," Lyric said. "Just another way that we've been maligned by angels. They're masters at controlling the narrative."

"He's right," Shy said to Lyric.

"Yeah," Deck affirmed.

"I can't go on a date today. I'm busy movin'," Shivaun told Lyric.

"How about tomorrow?" Lyric pressed.

"Maybe. Where would we go?"

"The River Road music festival at this ice house in New Braunfels?" When she didn't seem opposed to the idea, he embellished the plan. "We can watch people get drunk and fall down on the deck. Swim in the river. Make wildflowers."

"We can make wildflowers?" She looked as rapt as if she was under a spell.

He smiled. "You really are new. There's so much I can teach you."

"I'll bet," Deck said with undisguised disgust.

Ignoring her partner, Shivaun said, "Where's New Braunfels?"

"Texas." Lyric smiled seductively like Texas was the best destination in all the worlds eligible for a first date.

"Texas," she repeated. "Aye. Tomorrow."

CHAPTER NINE

SIMON SAYS

IT WAS UNUSUAL for Simon to keep Rosie waiting. She'd paced in his outer office for a full ten minutes while he finished a meeting with someone else. Glen sat calmly and watched silently for a time before saying, "Are you nervous about something?"

She stopped and stared at Glen for a couple of beats before resuming the pacing. "My project took a sharp left and headed south, but it wasn't my fault. Unless you're going to say that whatever happens on the boss's watch is her responsibility." She stopped and looked at Glen. "And it would be just like you to say that. You're such a goody two shoes."

He gaped for about two seconds before doubling over in peals of laughter.

"What's so funny?"

"What's so funny?!?" he repeated. "You called me a goody two shoes and then want to know what's funny?"

"Stow the misplaced pride in your bad boy history, husband. I'm talking about the fact that you're a stickler for rules. Sol-Nemamiah style leadership."

He'd grown serious at the reference. "I could do worse."

She was wiggling her head on her shoulders in an indecipherable way when Simon's door opened. Simon ushered a well-dressed middle-aged man past without even acknowledging Glen or Rosie.

"This is bad!" she whispered to Glen.

"What makes you think that?" Glen's tone was conversational.

"Because he didn't nod or make eye contact. Or *anything*!"

Simon had walked the visitor all the way to the front entrance of headquarters. When he stepped back in, he said something to his secretary then looked at Glen and Rosie for the first time.

As he walked past them, he said, "Come in. Tea service is on the way."

Behind Simon's back Rosie's eyes bugged and she mouthed, "Tea?"

Glen struck a meditation pose, hoping that she would interpret it as, "Relax!"

"Sit," Simon instructed as he sat in the big tufted leather swivel chair behind his desk.

Rosie noticed that there'd been some changes.

For one thing, there was an eighteen-inch bronze sculpture of a Hebridean sheep on a pedestal in the corner. She suspected it would be worth a fortune. The visitor chairs had also been recovered in a McCain hunting tartan that added to the feeling of luxurious masculine work-space.

"I see you've made some changes," Rosie said.

"What?" Simon looked around. "Oh." In answer, he simply turned a framed photo of Sorcha around to face Rosie.

"Well, she has good taste."

"She does." Simon's expression had softened just a tad. Enough so that Rosie wished they could keep him on the subject of his wife for a bit, have some tea and cakes, and get the hel out. Glen and Simon chatted about the ongoing struggle to control vampire in New York until the tea service arrived. When the door closed, Simon said, "Now to business."

"I take full responsibility for what's happened," Rosie volunteered, deciding that a preemptive offer of resignation was better than being fired. "And of course, I'll offer a letter of resignation and withdraw quietly."

Simon shook his head in tiny movements back and forth like he was completely lost. "What is it you're taking full responsibility for?" His face grew stern. "Gods almighty. Has one of the demons gone rogue?"

"No…" she began.

"ALL OF THEM?"

"Simon. The hunters are Black Swan to the core. They're not going 'rogue'. Have you been worrying about that?"

"Elora Rose, everybody in Black Swan, near and far, is worried about that. We're not going to, ah, decommission our own people. But on the other hand… It's a concern. A *big* concern."

She tried to remember if she'd ever heard of any Black Swan hunter being decommissioned. Then it hit her that it was a euphemism.

Rosie stood suddenly. "You mean *killed*!?!"

She was so stunned by the idea that such a thing had, apparently, been considered, even discussed, that she momentarily lost the tight control she kept on her emotions.

The floor beneath them rumbled as the Royal Doulton cups rattled in their saucers.

"Did you feel that?" Simon asked.

Suspecting that Rosie was the cause and wanting to cover for her, Glen said, "Feel what?"

"You're not killing my hunters," she said resolutely.

Simon glanced at Glen before pinning Rosie with the practiced gaze of a man who was used to telling people what they would and wouldn't do.

"Sit down, Elora Rose. Nobody said anything about killing. Your hunters are not in danger from Black Swan. In the event one of the Wild Bunch develops a problem, we have a secret weapon."

She took in a deep breath of relief and sat. Then replayed the rest of that sentence in her head. "What secret weapon?"

"You."

"Oh. I'm not killing my hunters either."

"No. Of course not. We're just running doomsday scenarios. It's what we do. The worst that could happen to them is exile from Loti."

"Why do you think there are going to be problems?"

Simon sighed. "I'm not making a prediction. I'm coming down on the side of optimism where the Wild Bunch is concerned. But we have to be realistic. They've undergone massive physiological changes. We don't know yet what changes have taken place in brain chemistry or neurological pathways. Their synapses may be firing in ways that are alien to us."

"To us?" Rosie said, beginning to feel like the target of a racist rant. "Does that include me?"

"Are you deliberately trying to be difficult today? No. It does not include you. We already know that your behavior is a hundred percent trustworthy."

"I see," she said without feeling conviction behind the words. She'd arrived at Simon's office feeling responsible, at least partially so, for people having been turned into demons. Whether that feeling was justified or not was debatable. But she would be leaving Simon's office feeling *very* protective of her baby demons.

"So what is it you're taking responsibility for?" Simon asked.

Realizing that the director was addressing her, she shook herself out of her daze and said, "Hmmm? Oh, for the whole, um, people turning demon thing."

"That's preposterous," Simon said. "Why would you take responsibility for that?"

Rosie looked at Glen. "I thought that's what leaders are supposed to do?"

"That's what you thought?" Simon actually rolled his eyes. "Well, put your offer to resign in that folder marked dumb ideas."

"Um…" she glanced around the director's desk like there might actually be a folder marked 'Dumb Ideas'.

"I asked you both here to talk about the possibility of having Rosie's hunters work with the vampire hunting division. It's been suggested that they could be an enormous help. Of course, Jefferson Unit came to mind as the ideal test case. What do you think?"

Glen and Rosie were both silent. Glen reached for a

mini éclair and popped it into his mouth. Rosie stirred her tea.

"The lack of enthusiasm is resounding," Simon said drily.

Glen cleared his throat. Intellectually he was all for anything that would end the threat of vampire. After all, he'd spent his whole life in that pursuit. First training to be a vampire hunter. Then acting as administrator of an elite unit, which made the notion of cat herding seem like child's play. But emotionally he was reluctant to see hundreds of years of history and tradition come to an end. He would never admit those private thoughts to anyone, but they were there. Under the surface.

"Of course, our goal is to end the vampire problem. That's always been the goal of Black Swan. I suppose I'm hesitating because, the last time we thought Dr. Monq had solved the problem, it turned out that the cure made the problem worse."

Simon nodded. "It's completely understandable that you're hesitant, given that history. We feel the same way, which is why we're proposing going slow. Rosie, what do you have to add?"

"Well, as you know, some of my hunters are ex-vampire hunters who were coaxed out of retirement because of the assurance that vampire hunting wasn't part of the gig. We can't do a bait and switch."

Simon turned the ghost of a smile toward Rosie. "Bait and switch. No. We can't do that. How many does that leave?"

"If you're asking how many hunters might be available for a test like that, I can't answer that question without talking to them. Like I said, they signed on for one thing. If they're willing to take on this other project, I'm willing to cooperate with the vampire hunting division. But it has to be voluntary."

Simon sat back and folded his hands together over his chest. "You've formed an attachment to the Wild Bunch." Rosie could see that Simon was evaluating her answer, looking for clues in expression, tone, and body language so that he could get the best read on her that was possible for a non-psychic.

"I don't know if attachment is the right word. I feel responsible for them. I *am* responsible for them."

"That's good news," Simon said. "And proves I picked

the right person for the job." He sat up and swiveled a quarter turn.

"It's not their fault, you know," Rosie blurted out. "It's hard enough to wake up alien without having Black Swan running 'doomsday scenarios'. You should be supporting them. Trying to help them adjust to their new way of... being."

Simon listened quietly. When he was sure Rosie was finished, he said, "I regret giving the impression that we mean your hunters harm, Elora Rose. Of course we're sympathetic to the fact that they're victims of a scientific experiment gone wrong. And we intend to support their successful transition in every way possible."

"I'm glad to hear that," she said.

Simon went on. "Of course we'd be deaf, dumb, and blind if we hadn't considered some of the implications and ramifications."

"Such as?" Rosie pressed.

"Black Swan now employs a team of sixteen demons, in addition to yourself, if you include yourself in that. It's Loti Dimension's own paranormal police force that we would never have dared to imagine. That's the enormous benefit for us. So far as the hunters go, we all hope that they will come to see this alteration as providential, because it goes without saying, there are *a lot* of advantages to being demon. There is a potential win win here."

After a brief pause, Rosie nodded slowly. "Okay. I see that."

"In your estimation, how are the hunters handling the change?"

"Psychologically?"

"Yes."

"Honestly? I've been surprised by their reactions. I'd sort of expected to see more emotional turmoil, but if anybody is having a problem they're covering really well. They're giving the appearance of being fine with it. Even, as you said, focusing on the benefits."

"Maybe the change in their physiology assisted their outlook?"

"Maybe. I will be keeping an eye out for depression. Or whatever." She looked over at Glen, who'd been extraordinarily quiet. "But I won't be sending them to Monq for counseling. He's got a conflict of interest."

Simon nodded. "He does. You're right. If anybody needs counseling, they can come here and see Dr. Tincture."

"Okay."

"So what about the joint vampire hunting initiative?"

"Now it's an initiative? I thought you were proposing a test."

"Yes. A test that, if successful, will become an initiative. Can I expect cooperation between your divisions?"

"If Glen wants to do this, I'll talk to my hunters. Oh, by the way, I had everybody move to Hunter Abbey. There's no point in maintaining separate residences because they can commute to work really, um, fast."

Simon barked out a laugh. "Commute. Funny. Well, thank you for minding the company purse. We'll get rid of the properties since they're no longer needed." He looked at Rosie. "So. They're all living at your Abbey?"

"My Abbey?" Her eyes widened.

"You know what I mean," Simon said.

"Yeah. Headquarters is also home, but I told them they're welcome to have as many private homes as they want and can afford, um, anywhere they want."

"And by anywhere, you mean…"

"Loti or elsewhere."

Simon frowned. "You encouraged the Wild Bunch to acquire off world residences?"

"I didn't encourage anything. I gave them that option. Like you said, there are advantages to being demon. Pointing out those advantages may be what's helping to get them past the shock of transforming into a completely different species."

"Hope you know what you're doing."

"Me, too."

"Glen," Simon said, "are you in for a test of demon vampire hunters?"

Glen shrugged, but didn't look happy. "Sure. I guess."

"Am I hearing reservations?"

"Well," Glen paused, wanting to be sure he was careful with his words, "you're worried about the psychological effect of all this on Rosie's hunters. I'm concerned about the psychological effect on *my* hunters. Their skills are unparalleled when compared to other people, but not when compared to demons. If they take a demon on patrol, and it appears they're no longer needed by Black

Swan, how will they react to that? Because I suspect the reaction will be first depression, then trying to decide what else to do with their lives.

"The first test is pretty much a step off that cliff because the hunters talk to each other. Within a couple of hours all the hunters everywhere on Earth are going to know. Are we ready to give up centuries' worth of effort that's gone into the current crop of vampire hunters?

"And I can't help but be reminded of the last time we were sure we didn't need vampire hunters anymore. We dismantled way too fast and were caught unprepared when the new mutation surged. We didn't foresee that. Couldn't have foreseen that. What else is out there that we don't foresee?"

Simon had listened intently. He had enormous respect for Glen, though he was decades younger, and had often thought that if he was forced to name a replacement, Glen's was the only name that would come to mind.

"Well said, Sovereign," Simon began. "What do you recommend?"

"I hate to be the guy who presents problems with no solution. But there it is. Honestly, you want to know what

I think will happen?"

"I do," said Simon.

"I think my hunters will ask for the serum the Wild Bunch took."

Simon sucked a full breath in through his nostrils. "That's not something we're prepared to do."

"You know, that was my first reaction when Monq raised the possibility. I said the same thing to him only, perhaps, with less civility.

"But since then I've had time to really think it over. I was reacting in anger to the fact that we made victims of our own people by not giving them a choice in the matter. There's a big difference between having an irrevocable condition foisted upon you and volunteering after being presented all the information. Think about giving my hunters that choice. They're more than capable of weighing the pros and cons and deciding for themselves."

Simon opened his mouth to speak, but Glen interrupted. "Before you order a test or get further into initiative planning, I'm asking you to really consider this. We could rid Loti Dimension of both outside agitators *and* vampire. Isn't that what we're supposed to be about? I'm having a hard time understanding why we wouldn't want to use the tools at our disposal. It would be like having stakes in reserve, but telling my people they have to go hunting without them."

Glen saw that something in that last spoken sentence caused a moment of indecision to flicker in Simon's eyes.

"So you're saying we'd shut down the vampire hunter program because another generation of hunters would never be needed. That these hunters would have the satisfaction of ridding us of vampire once and for all and would be made demon as a, what, reward?"

Glen nodded. "They might look at it that way. We won't know unless we ask."

Simon's gaze flitted toward Rosie to see what her reaction was. Seeing nothing there, his attention returned to Glen. "Let me think about this for a couple of days. Maybe talk to some of the people I respect most."

"That's all I can ask," Glen said.

"Very well. That's all for now."

Glen and Rosie stood at Simon's polite dismissal and said their goodbyes. Rosie snapped the handcuffs on Glen to make sure she didn't lose him in the passes on the return trip to Jefferson Unit, where they would, no doubt, have a more private sharing of their thoughts on Glen's change of heart and his proposal to Simon.

EPILOGUE

WORKING IN THE LAB LATE ONE NIGHT

TORN AND SHER decided they would search for a world with a copy of her New Forest home, but uninhabited. And there they would build the home they'd share away from the Abbey. Sher wanted to model it after the royal family's hunting cottage. Torrent Finngarick was happy when Sheridan O'Malley was happy.

BRYCE PALADINO WAS ONE of Monq's brightest assistants. She'd been living at Jefferson Unit and working in the lab since graduating M.I.T. with a doctorate in biomedical engineering ten years before.

Prior to the Deliverance project, she'd worked on developing nutritional supplements for the vampire hunters. In other words, her field of specialization was performance enhancers. It had been rewarding to know that the hunters were at their very best. She took pride in knowing that, in some way, she helped give them a fighting chance against carriers of the vampire virus. But nothing could compare with having been instrumental in developing a formula that actually turned people into demons.

The very idea of it sounded more like primitive folklore than modern science. But then vampirism was primitive folklore reinterpreted by modern science in practical terms.

Knowing that she could turn an ordinary person into a demon with an injection was… well, god like.

So, when she overheard Monq telling his right hand that they were probably going to be ordered to scrap the entire project, which would include destroying every journal note and scrap of evidence, she actually felt her soul recoil.

They couldn't possibly destroy the stuff of fantasy. It struck Bryce that even carrying on a discussion about the prospect of such a heinous deed was evil. And she knew in an instant what she had to do.

No one should have the right to 'undo' scientific progress. Not even Black Swan. Not even if they conceived of it and funded it.

She shook her head without realizing she was doing it. Indeed. She would rescue the project including the how-to's of recreation.

Once that decision was made, it was a short distance in her mind to mulling over practical applications. After all, wouldn't people be willing to pay millions, even billions, for a greatly extended life and a virtual ticket that enabled them to slip dimensions at will? No external devices necessary?

WHEN IT CAME to the hunter division, Black Swan had always been concerned with more than physical training and academics. Words like character, honor, ethics, morality, and the like were commonly heard in class-rooms, training rooms, on the playing field, and in Chamber gatherings.

Long before the vampire hunters were knighted, they'd proven themselves to be exceptional. Teachers were charged with keeping an eye out for character flaws during the training years. If a student proved to have a less than stellar understanding of the standards and principles of Black Swan, they were released and returned home. It didn't happen often because recruiters had a keen eye for prospects. But it did happen.

All that is to say that nothing of the sort could be said about other personnel. Before being hired in any capacity, potential employees had to pass a test indicating satisfactory confidentiality scores and they had to take an oath pledging confidentiality. But their personal morals were not subject to the same intense scrutiny as future knights.

That, combined with Bryce's complete freedom of access to everything on the science level, was what made it easy for her to copy everything onto a thimble drive. In addition she took three vials of the serum and a half vial of the original sample of demon blood collected from Deliverance. Those she stored in a sports drink container in the refrigerator in her apartment.

When she had days off, she would look for a place of her own in the city. The sort of place that featured a doorman and key entry elevators. Since she'd banked her most excellent salary for a decade and spent very little, she could afford to live anywhere. She'd store the fruit of her industrial espionage there until she'd decided how to proceed.

Author's Notes:

I sincerely hope you enjoyed reading *Irish War Cry*.

If asked the party question about what superpower I'd like, I might say elf turned demon wouldn't be bad. What could be wrong with being permanently young and so gorgeous you could stop traffic, incredibly strong and fast, able to freely move between dimensions like a demigod, quasi-immortal, and essentially invincible? Yes. Please.

I don't know if this will eventually mean that the last knight that will ever be recruited for Black Swan has already been recruited. We'll have to see where the story goes.

Meanwhile, there are fifteen new demons with adventures on the horizon and each one may end up with a story to tell.

Reviews are enormously helpful to me. Please take the time to follow a link back to the book you've just read and post your thoughts. A few words is often as powerful as many.

Victoria Danann

NEW YORK TIMES and USA TODAY BESTSELLING AUTHOR

SUBSCRIBE TO MY MAIL LIST Be first to know...
eepurl.com/wRE3T

Victoria's Website
www.victoriadanann.com

Victoria's Facebook Page
facebook.com/victoriadanannbooks

Twitter
twitter.com/vdanann

Pinterest
pinterest.com/vdanann

Victoria's Facebook Fan Group
facebook.com/groups/772083312865721

Links to all Victoria's books can be found here...
www.VictoriaDanann.com

ALSO BY VICTORIA DANANN

THE KNIGHTS OF BLACK SWAN

Knights of Black Swan 1, My Familiar Stranger

Knights of Black Swan 2, The Witch's Dream

Knights of Black Swan 3, A Summoner's Tale

Knights of Black Swan 4, Moonlight

Knights of Black Swan 5, Gathering Storm

Knights of Black Swan 6, A Tale of Two Kingdoms

Knights of Black Swan 7, Solomon's Sieve

Knights of Black Swan 8, Vampire Hunter

Knights of Black Swan 9, Journey Man

Knights of Black Swan 10, Falcon

Knights of Black Swan 11, Jax

Knights of Black Swan 12, Deliverance

ORDER OF THE BLACK SWAN D.I.T.

D.I.T. 1, Simon Says

D.I.T. 2, Finngarick

D.I.T. 3, Irish War Cry

D.I.T. 4, The Wild Hunt

ORDER OF THE BLACK SWAN NOVELS

Black Swan Novel, Prince of Demons

THE HYBRIDS

Exiled 1, CARNAL

Exiled 2, CRAVE

Exiled 3, CHARMING

THE WEREWOLVES

New Scotia Pack 1, Shield Wolf: Liulf

New Scotia Pack 2, Wolf Lover: Konochur

New Scotia Pack 3, Fire Wolf: Cinaed

New Scotia Pack 4, Brandish

THE WITCHES OF WIMBERLEY

Witches of Wimberley 1, Willem

CONTEMPORARY ROMANCE

SSMC Austin, TX, Book 1, Two Princes

SSMC Austin, TX, Book 2, The Biker's Brother

SSMC Austin, TX, Book 3, Nomad

SSMC Austin, TX, Book 4, Devil's Marker

SSMC Austin, TX, Book 5, Roadhouse

Made in the USA
Columbia, SC
05 December 2017